G000125991

Cape Misfortune

or

The Disappearance of Cassandra Dollar

By Henry Anderson

ALL RIGHTS RESERVED

Publisher's Note:

This is a work of fiction. All names, characters, places, and events are the work of the author's imagination.

Any resemblance to real persons, places, or events is coincidental.

Solstice Publishing - www.solsticepublishing.com

To Tania

Prologue

My parents loved the land and it repaid their kindness with the sweet, unlikely bounty of an ocean's shore.

No living thing on our farm was untouched by the salt breeze that blew in off the water. It crossed the sloping fruit orchards, caressed our fertile fields then climbed up high into the rocky hills to rustle the pines.

I can recall every acre in my mind's eye. Every meadow and field blossomed with purpose and beauty. I see such bright images when I close my eyes. They are pictures of an Eden from which I will forever be exiled.

Mom and Dad had their daughters working from a young age. We could tell the difference between twenty different types of manure before either of us could string sentences together.

We kept dairy goats, milk cows, horses, chickens, two working dogs, and a hog we named Whistler.

There were always chores to do. My earliest memory is of my mom teaching us to milk the family dairy cow before breakfast. How the metal bucket clanged with each squirt.

Dad put up long fences to keep the animals in their pastures. We held the posts as he drove them into the earth. Then we shepherded beasts between those newly enclosed spaces. In spring, the cows calved. In fall, we weened those children from their anguished mothers.

On school vacations we rose before the sun did, worked in the fields, or mucked out stables, coming home caked in mud and smelling of the farmyard. We were asleep in our beds before the sun sank into the sea.

Some days, our family rode horses over the high places too steep and rocky for a vehicle. Up high, we felt a sacred connection between land, sea, and air. Those upland pastures were holy places where each thought could quickly become a prayer that flew into the sky.

I remember.

The first European settlers called our farm "Preiselbeeren" - German for cranberries – in honor of the evergreen, dwarf shrub that flourished in our strange, coastal micro-climate. Moist, salty air blowing in from the ocean turned our sandy soil acid. The ground was watered by coastal rain.

When I hear the word *home*, I see our house - a wooden shack with a brick chimney and iron roof just a stone's throw from the shore. It was derelict when my parents bought the farm - a stubborn survivor of Pacific rain and wind. Mom and Dad lived in a tent while they fitted it with a new metal roof and floorboards.

My twin sister, Agata, called our home *the Prize*.

"Because that's what it feels like," she said, when my mom asked why. That's what we called it ever after.

Growing up I always felt there was something ancient about the place. Pieces fell off it and every big rainstorm something leaked.

In the fall of each year, Dad flooded our cranberry bogs. Islands of the rich red fruit, lighter than the vines they grew on, floated up to the surface and lay on the face of the water.

We pulled on waders and pushed machines with whirring arms called "beaters" that knocked the berries off their vines. Later, a truck backed onto the bogs and sucked up the bobbing dark-red harvest.

We would go home tired, but satisfied.

Aggie and I shared a bedroom that looked out onto an orchard of pear, cherry and plum trees sloping to the water's edge. I imagined the hill was a giant touching its head to the ground in worship of the ocean which, through the window, was a long line of ever-changing light and color.

Every night, we were lulled to sleep by the roar of the angry surf fighting a never-ending battle with the rocky cliffs. The rat-a-tat-tat of rain on the window pane often accompanied it. In the darkness of our bedroom, it became almost like a tune – a lullaby from an orchestra across the sea.

The ocean was always part of our life. Most Sundays, after church, our family walked down to the beach. My grandma, widowed a few weeks before we were born, made ice cream in a wooden pail.

There were no sandy beaches on our little stretch of the headland. That was not how the land rolled. We climbed down steps carved out of a volcanic cliff to the horseshoe-shaped Wish Bay – a cauldron of seething water. Here, rocks were weathered by untold years of rain and surf. The bay was dominated by Needle Rock, a tall, tapering stack a quarter mile off-shore.

"A forgotten god flipping us a giant middle finger," my grandma once said, to no one in particular.

The ocean was a wild, massive neighbor; brutal but captivating. A mix of pressure systems off the coast made for high waves. Sometimes, the surf threw out stones big enough to take your eye out, or a riptide strong enough to drag you under permanently.

Most local Cape folk find the water too cold and untrustworthy to swim at any time of year. But I always loved that fierce cauldron of muscular light. I suppose you find comfort where you can get it.

While the adults read the newspaper, or dozed, Aggie and I splashed around in sparkling rock pools, filled with a mixture of river and seawater. We trampled over brightly-colored algae and seaweed with our knives and buckets looking for the little, bluish-black, bay mussels or the larger, California, surf variety you may find in the rocky crevices or overhangs of the Cape coast.

The shells were encrusted with barnacles but there was good meat inside. Grandma usually served them up in a chowder that night.

Although I'm a local, I have to admit Cape Misfortune is not a tourist trap. The Cape has more than its fair share of extreme weather. Our circle of treacherous headland got its name from ships getting smashed against the rocks. But the major loss of life was due to a particular phenomenon - fog.

In 1850, the United States Corps of Engineers built a lighthouse on a protruding sea stack a mile out to sea. They called it **"Narwak"** – because of the noise big waves made against the rock.

Now and then, a big fog rolled in from the ocean. The settlers called it the **"Nebel"**, their home country's word for 'fog.' Over the years it morphed into "weasel," which was how everyone described the obliterating white-outs that periodically hit us.

Sometimes the Weasel came in as we had our Sunday picnic on the rocks. The Dollars packed up their gear as a silent cloud crept over the water, with the nonchalant but practiced stealth of an old predator.

My sister swore she could hear it hiss when it made landfall.

"This place is a fog factory," my dad would say, shaking his head.

It sneaked over the rocks, climbed the cliffs and stayed for…well, as long as it liked. The Weasel played by its own rules. Sometimes it was gone in minutes; other times it loitered for hours in our bogs and fields. It was like the dispossessed ghost of a lost landscape.

In those times, the land was blind, and nothing moved. The cows and goats gathered in silent groups. We kept the doors shut and didn't look out of the window.

Cape people tried to make the best of things and held a yearly fog festival in Valkyrie, Cape Misfortune's increasingly run-down town. But we all knew it was something to be faced.

On fog-free summer evenings, my grandmother sat on the Prize's back porch watching the sunset and drinking cranberry wine. She was usually on her own. The land around the back was untended and, as a result, thronged with bats. Mom claimed the swooping invaders ate thousands of bugs and saved us big bucks on insecticide.

One year, when we were older, and things were getting easier for us money-wise, Dad bought an old hot tub from a neighbor which he installed on the porch. It was a wooden, hexagonal affair. My parents never used it. But we did.

Two or three days after it arrived, Aggie and I sat in bubbling water either side of Grandma and watched the sun disappear behind the hills. She had brought out homemade cranberry cookies to lure my sister and me onto her porch. Grandma sipped cranberry wine while we drank the juice. Funny thing was, none of us ever got sick of those berries.

We watched bats arrive from upland pines, navigating between dogwood and crabapple trees in search of insects for their supper.

"Bats," my grandma said. "Are considered lucky on the Cape. They keep away other creatures with wings. And I'm not talking about birds."

That was a typical comment of hers. Over time, we came to learn the many strange, unofficial histories of our headland as we sat in the tub.

Grandma Dollar had married an Italian immigrant. But she was Cape German. Her name was Odessa. She had a long face and large, violet eyes that took in most things. While she loved those strange early tales, she tried to inject a note of scorn. It was difficult to be skeptical in a bat-haunted sunset sitting in bubbling water.

The first Europeans on Cape Misfortune came for coal, timber and fishing but the fog played with them, Grandma said. Things went missing. Animals mainly but, eventually, people too. And ships. The rocky headland earned its name of Kap Schicksal, Cape Misfortune, early. Back then, people blamed the disappearances on old superstitions like the fae, the little creatures with white wings who flew in from hidden islands beyond the fog. Or the Tatzelwurm, a cat-headed snake who swallowed their victims whole. They were commanded by Krampus, a goat-legged mischief maker.

"Is he for real?" Aggie asked.

"People believe in him. That makes him real."

Grandma told us stories of the dead turning up in people's front gardens during the fog, some freshly disappeared, others missing for years. Also lost fishermen who claimed to have seen the Isle of the Dead appearing out of the fog. Oddest of all were strangers who claimed they were from the Cape, born and bred, but had magically disappeared from everyone's memory. Often there were tales of monsters - beasts the size of whales crawling out of the sea in Wish Bay.

Aggie asked why there weren't any books about it.

"No one ever wrote any of it down," Grandma said. "For fear of sounding foolish."

A month later, a few days before she passed on, we sat in the tub with Grandma, as we did every night now. This time we watched the fog creep across our land like an enemy soldier.

"Here comes the Weasel," Grandma said, in her slight Cape German accent. "Time to go in, ladies."

Aggie looked at Grandma.

"What about a tale?"

Aggie was my identical twin, we were both dark-haired and olive-skinned, but her features were a little more delicate than mine.

Grandma thought for a moment.

"Your great-great aunt Ursula, maybe more greats – I'm not sure - got into some bother in the old times. One foggy afternoon, blue-skinned fae with pools of liquid silver for eyes and skin-flaps for wings swooped out of the fog and snatched Ursula's baby daughter, Annika. Poor Ursula ran around shouting out her child's name. But there was no answer."

Grandma took a sip of wine.

"That evening, Ursula took a musket from her house and put a jar of honey beside a flaming torch on the beach."

"The fae like honey?" Aggie asked.

Grandma took a cookie from a plate and crunched on it.

"Oh yeah. When it came, the fae still carried poor baby Annika on its back. Ursula had one shot and had to make it count. She got the creature between the eyes. The fae fell to a few feet over the ground. But it recovered itself and smiled at Ursula. Then it grabbed the honey and flew away, satisfied."

"How come?"

"It was already dead."

"That doesn't make sense," Aggie said.

"Some fae cheat death by drinking a potion called manna, which kept them alive for a while."

"How long?" Aggie asked.

"A year and a day. No more, no less."

"That's not fair," I said.

"What a depressing story, Grandma," Aggie said.

"Well, they don't call this place Cape Misfortune for nothing. Sadly, the story isn't finished. It got worse. Word was little Annika had cut herself on a geschank. That's a knife with a curse written on the blade. The fae forge them. Get cut and you become a slave to the knife's maker. There was no chance of getting her back."

Grandma leaned over the side of the tub and poured herself another glass of wine.

"They strung Ursula up on the crossroads outside Valkyrie town. She never said a word. Guess people wouldn't have paid much heed to what a woman said in those days, anyway."

The fog was pouring through the trees into the wasteland.

"Bad things always happen in the fog," I said.

"The fog isn't good or bad. It was men that lynched Ursula. Folks around here use the Weasel for their own reasons."

Our little party was silent for a while.

"Did I ever tell you about the Stinkwolf?" Grandma asked. "His breath was so bad it could knock you out from twenty paces."

We laughed.

The fog oozed over the meadow a few yards ahead of us.

Grandma held up her glass and saluted it.

"Great Aunt Ursula should have argued her case. But she blamed herself. Thought she deserved death for letting Annika get cut, maybe."

As she spoke, tendrils of fog crept up the porch steps. Soon we were enclosed in the Weasel's cold, moist embrace.

"Which one of you girls said they want to be a deputy?" Grandma asked.

"Me," Aggie said.

"Your Grandpa Dollar wore a star for a while. He said you have to tell it straight on the Cape. Or you get lost."

She stood up in the tub, the water streaming from her body.

"He also thought folks around here sometimes use the Weasel to go missing. My two cents? Nobody ever really disappears. Because the missing know where they are, even if no one else can see them."

She was smart, my grandmother. One day she had breath and vitality. The next she was gone.

A few years later, on a foggy morning in the balmy season, when the September and October storms ease up a little, tragedy found our family.

The weasel fog had arrived the previous night. I was checking my phone for confirmation the school bus would be canceled.

Aggie had taken Grandma's old bedroom. She had not come downstairs yet.

My parents ate their breakfast and watched the local news.

My mother was a wiry, outdoor type. Her fine hair was usually pulled back in a ponytail, ready for a day's work outside. My father was heavy set and dark-haired. He had a humorous disposition, like his mother, until now.

Mom called up to Aggie a few times. Dad frowned. He went upstairs and knocked on Aggie's door. Mom joined him. She tried the handle. After a minute of knocking and yelling, Dad charged the door with his shoulder.

The room was empty. The windows were closed.

Mom checked in Grandma's old chest of drawers while Dad looked under the bed.

"She may have fallen over in the fog," Mom said. "Maybe she went to feed the chickens. Or Whistler. Or to milk Henrietta. She could be somewhere out there now, hurt."

Dad ran down the stairs and out into the mist.

"Aggie! Aggie!" we heard him shout.

We had searched the house. Mom stood beside the phone on the hall table. Her green eyes already looked distant.

Dad came in and shook his head.

Mom picked the receiver up. Her hand shook, but her voice was steady.

"My name is Angela Dollar. My daughter, Agata, is missing. She is fourteen years old."

A deputy from the Sheriff's Office arrived a half hour later, on foot.

Buzz Everett was tall, wide-faced and broad-shouldered. He had been in Mom's year at high school. He sometimes came to our family barbecues. Aggie and I called him 'Uncle Buzz.' He was breathing hard today. His wavy, blonde hair fell across his forehead.

He asked some questions. Were clothes missing from Aggie's room? Has she been acting strangely? Could they think of anyone who might want to abduct her?

That last question made my parents recoil.

"We'll get everyone we can out searching, once the fog clears," Buzz said.

"Is it the Weasel?" I said.

"No, that's a fairy-tale, honey." Buzz smiled.

He didn't look convinced, though.

Most of the Venice County Sheriff's Office came to the house that day.

When the fog cleared, there was a search.

A local TV crew arrived. A journalist named Carol Severin asked for an interview. Buzz advised Mom and Dad to make a statement, an appeal to the kidnapper. And so it went on. The truth that she might be gone forever hitting us in increasing waves.

A week later, my mom lay beside me on my bed knocked out by grief and alcohol. Rain tapped on the window. Almost a tune. I dozed. Then I heard radio static.

I looked outside. Curls of fog were rubbing up against the window glass like a cat.

Someone had given us walkie-talkies for Christmas. We used them a couple of times and then forgot them. Mine lay under a pile of stuff in my closet. I picked it up.

I wasn't even sure it was switched on.

"Cassandra?" Aggie asked.

I pressed the talk button.

"Aggie, where are you?"

"Gone."

"Aggie, please come back. We're all frightened."

A buzz of static was followed by silence.

Mom didn't do much except cry now. Often, she knelt on the kitchen floor, making the noises a body makes when despair takes over. Dad would get down and hold her, and they would clutch each other in silent agony like that. Grief flowed through the Prize like a river.

After a while, the cops stopped calling every day. Our house became a mostly silent place. My Mom started sleeping in Aggie's room, on her own.

Dad neglected the farm and started driving to Valkyrie. I heard later he was asking questions about Aggie and other people who had gone missing.

Occasionally, he spoke to invisible people in the attic.

After a couple of months Buzz came by.

"Ronnie, you've got to stop going around town upsetting people. Pop Wessendorf says you are harassing his family. And the Coffi H.Q. in Valkyrie has complained about you asking people questions outside the building."

"They know something about Aggie," my dad said. "Not one of them will talk to me, Buzz."

"Do you have proof of any wrongdoing?"

My dad handed him a bulging, cardboard file.

"It's big, Buzz. A lot of people involved. Local people. Hank Frederson, maybe."

Buzz sighed.

"I'll check it out. But you need to stop bothering people."

A month later, Buzz Everett went missing himself - during a fog. A hiker found his abandoned patrol car in the salt marshes south of Valkyrie. He was a keen rock climber. They found a wrist watch and some of his climbing gear at the bottom of the cliffs.

No one from the Sheriff's Office came round after that.

A psychiatrist named Alvarez told the County District Medical Examiner that Buzz was a recently divorced workaholic who probably took his own life.

Dad talked to himself more than other people now.

A few days after Buzz disappeared, my father left his empty truck on the cliff overlooking Wish Bay. One day he was there, the next he wasn't. His body was never found.

Mom didn't discuss it with me. In fact, we hardly said anything to each other after that.

I finished high school, tended bar and worked on other people's farms. Mom said she was selling the Prize to a local entrepreneur who was thinking of building houses on it.

I started drinking heavily.

When seasonal work got scarce, I came back to Cape Misfortune and camped out in our old house.

The windows of the Prize were boarded up and the rooms empty. The cranberry bogs were so choked with tall weeds that they would have been called a fire hazard if anybody bothered to inspect them.

I slept on an old, mouse-eaten mattress on the landing. Sometimes, I heard voices in the wind as I lay awake at night. I would walk to the back porch and watch shadows move amongst the swaying weeds. It would have been spooky if I had cared enough.

One morning a young, Venice County deputy pushed the front door open, hand resting on his pistol. He had dark brown hair and a pale, handsome face, almost ruined by a mustache. He ran his eyes over me and took in the derelict hallway.

I made a half-hearted attempt to fix my hair.

"The old sign outside says Preiselbeeren," he said, "That's German, right?"

"It means cranberries."

"My folks are Polish. Do you know you're staying in a building that's not fit for habitation?"

"I grew up here."

"Well, now you need to pack up your stuff and leave."

"I don't have anywhere to go."

"You're committing criminal trespass. The house belongs to someone else. Also, it isn't safe."

"Don't you have any real criminals to go after, Officer?"

The young deputy smiled.

"You're committing a Class A misdemeanor. That's a year in jail. Real enough for you?"

I couldn't think of anything to say to that, so I didn't. He looked at the empty beer bottles.

"Why d'you come back here? You a substance abuser?"

I shook my head.

'You got any family you can stay with?"

"Do you think I'd be here if I did?"

'That's odd. Because it was your mother who called the Sheriff's Office to find out where you are. She's worried about you."

"We don't talk much."

"You know there's a temporary accommodation shelter in Valkyrie?"

He drove me there in his patrol car.

His name was Boone Washienko.

Reader, I married him. I went to the State Police Academy and learned how to tend to the human farm. I passed the background check, the psychological exam, and no one mentioned Dad or Aggie to me.

My first shift Sergeant did, though.

The old-fashioned, felt hat on my head made me feel like an old-style Girl Scout. A fur-collared, waterproof duty jacket, a white shirt, blue necktie and gray pants with a black stripe down the side finished the ensemble.

The little Sheriff's Office substation stood on a cliff overlooking Wish Bay. It looked like a discarded shoebox. Officers called my new workplace 'Needle Rock' in honor of the skinny, sea stack that pointed out of the ocean behind it.

I pushed the glass door. It opened into a small, functional room. Bulging stacks of paper and files covered several desks. Missing persons posters filled most of the notice boards.

Sergeant Ann Ambrose sat behind the middle desk. She was a large woman, black, maybe in her early fifties, and had a long chin.

"I understand you actually asked to be assigned to Cape Misfortune, is that right?"

"Yes, ma'am."

"I've been on the job a long while and that's a first. I'm from Venice City - the mainland as you guys call it. You didn't fancy cutting your teeth somewhere with more people?"

"No. I was raised around here. I hope my local knowledge will be useful."

"You okay arresting friends or family? People you knew in high school?"

"If I have to."

"You now reside in Venice City with another deputy?"

"Deputy Washienko. My husband."

Sergeant Ambrose opened one of the many folders on her desk.

"Your father and sister went missing from Cape Misfortune. Is that right?"

"That's correct."

She looked me in the eye.

"Did you become a police officer to try and find them?"

"No."

"I'm sorry for your loss but you're not one of these people who believe in the...what is the ridiculous name local people call it?"

"The Weasel. No, ma'am, I don't."

"Good, it's just fog. Anyone who says otherwise isn't fit to wear that uniform you currently have on. You hear me?"

"Loud and clear, ma'am."

Ann studied me for a second.

"I looked up your sister's case. I remember it. I came to your house. Buzz Everett got obsessed with it. You know he killed himself?"

"They didn't find a body. But, yes, it looked like suicide."

Ann sighed.

"Just don't become a Cape Misfortune crazy, Cassandra."

She took a bunch of keys from her desk drawer.

"Let's go on patrol."

A small garage beside the station housed a big, Ford Interceptor patrol car with Venice County markings.

"You want to drive first, or last?" Ann asked.

"First, I guess."

The arrow-straight Seven Mile Lane cut through a perpetually overcast landscape of salt marshes.

"You may patrol with a partner occasionally," Ann said. "But budget cuts mean you'll mostly be on your own. That means liaising with other officers before you attend a crime where more than one officer is needed."

"Yes, ma'am."

Ann opened the mobile computer unit, a chunky, beefed-up laptop mounted on a console between the seats.

A gas station went past. Ann tapped a few keys.

"The villages around here are pretty small," Ann said. "But I suppose you'd know that."

"Yes, ma'am."

"In Valkyrie, we share jurisdiction with the local, town cops. They're mostly okay when you get to know them. We're going there now."

The early pioneers had named Valkyrie after a village in Bohemia. The mascot on the road sign was a grey wolf. Maybe the Stinkwolf Grandma talked about, though I doubt anyone would admit it.

They had settled here to make a utopia.

We drove into town, passing lines of empty, rundown houses before parking on the waterfront. The natural harbor Valkyrie grew up around had a glockenspiel clock tower that still chimed the hour a few yards from the main pier.

Ann looked out at the rocky waterfront. A light rain stippled the ocean water.

"No tourists or young families. This old rock can't seem to catch a break."

"I went to high school here," I said. "It's getting worse."

Valkyrie had once been a major destination for passenger ships and cargo liners. Now it was unsuccessfully transitioning into a tourist resort.

"Let's head north, Deputy."

We took the winding beach road towards Slaughter Lake, a brooding expanse that glittered when the clouds relented, parting to allow an occasional ray of sun. Then we passed into the tree-shaded Valkyrie State Park - a mass of green foliage that covered half the Cape. Ann pointed out hiking trails, birdwatching and fishing spots.

"We've busted a few meth labs and pot farms in here. It's big and under-policed, so local felons use it for burying stuff, too. You'll get to know them. A surprising amount goes on in these woods."

"Right."

She hesitated.

"There have been a few missing person reports in the Devil's Hollow area."

The radio crackled.

"Report of a 1215 in Wish Bay," a dispatcher said.

Venice used idiosyncratic twelve codes. I had spent a couple of afternoons learning them. Boone had tested me afterwards. This meant a disturbance of the peace.

I turned the siren on and we sped south across the headland.

There was no vehicle access to Wish Bay's beach, so we parked above the cliffs and hurried down steps cut into dark, basalt rock.

I remembered this place from before Aggie went missing. Our family had loved it here. Now it was raining. Cold and insistent. Birdsong from the cliff was just audible above the surf.

The Keyhole Rock, named after its roughly keyhole-shaped middle, had stood twenty feet high and been the pride of the beach. Now the ancient, noble presence lay on its side, broken at the base. The break looked new. There were shards of loose rock scattered around.

The wind started to gust, and the salt breeze from the surf stung our eyes.

"You know what this is?" Ann asked.

"The Keyhole Rock. Sacred to the Shell tribe."

"And the Cape Misfortune tourist board."

"Brute force. Must have taken a few people," I said. "They must have rocked it."

Ann nodded. Her cell phone rang.

I saw a knife with a rusty blade lying in a nearby rock pool. I didn't pick it up.

Ann spoke on her phone for a minute.

"Well, the good news is Investigations is sending a detective over. The bad news? They won't be here until tomorrow morning, at the earliest. There's a storm coming. It won't be safe down here."

"Good evening, Officers," a voice said, behind us.

My husband walked over.

"Good evening, Boone," Ann said. 'I'm heading up to interview our witness, Frau Postulart. Her house overlooks the bay. She's a 911 junkie."

"Why would anyone knock a rock over?" I said.

Boone and Ann exchanged a look.

"See if you turn anything up, Cassandra, then call it a day and get out of this rain," Ann said.

We watched her climb the steps. The sun was setting over the Pacific, coloring the fast-moving storm clouds heading towards us, purple and orange.

"You two know something about this, don't you?" I asked

Boone nodded.

"Someone's been destroying Cape landmarks."

"Why would anyone do that?"

He shrugged.

"Why does anyone do anything? For kicks, I suppose."

"This took organization. There has to be more to it than that."

He looked at his feet.

"There are plenty of local, conspiracy theories on the Internet. The Coffi Corporation has asked for planning permission to build a natural gas pipe that will end up here in Wish Bay."

"Here?"

Boone shrugged.

"Yeah. It will take gas from Canada, then all points south to a new port where we're standing. Then ship it out to foreign countries. It will bring much-needed cash to the county."

"So what does knocking down an old stone achieve?"

"One less landmark. Makes the area easier to develop."

The broken keyhole rock was already half-submerged in foaming surf, rocking gently back and forth in the incoming tide.

"Let's get out of here and avoid being killed in the storm," I said.

"Good idea."

But first Boone closed his arms around me, and we kissed. Our hats fell off, and we had to chase them over the rocks.

Halfway up the cliff steps, Boone stopped.

"My mom brought my sister and me here to see the minus tide, once. That's when an early spring tide goes out further than usual. Mom claimed some nights you could see a hidden ghost road through an ancient forest."

"Did she say where the road went to?"

"The Otherworld, the Isle of the Dead. She loved all that hoodoo stuff. I think she started to believe it to try and fit in here. You know how weird you Cape folk are."

"Yeah, I had a lecture from the Sarge about that."

The wind buffeted us as we climbed to the top. I looked down on the Bay. The sun had gone below the horizon. The sea was a dark, seething mass.

Ann had gone home.

Boone and I made out on one of the desks in the substation while the wind screamed through nearby trees and power lines.

It felt like a new life had begun.

Part One: Cape Misfortune

Chapter One
Bang

The fog was so bad I couldn't see the painted line on the side of the road. But I felt the tires vibrate on the asphalt. That would change if the car strayed off-road into the marsh.

Seven Mile Lane is dead straight. Just drive steady, I thought. The speedometer said I was doing fifteen miles an hour. It felt faster.

I passed the spot where a detachment of cavalry volunteers went missing during the Civil War. The whole Cape heard gunfire and screaming, my Grandma claimed.

"Someone should have told them. If you get lost in the fog, avoid hag stones – big rocks with holes in them. They appear out of nowhere. If you go through, they take you straight to the Isle of the Dead.

"And, if you're near Slaughter Lake, watch out for storm maidens - shape thieves who jump out of the water and rip the skin off your body so they can take human form."

My history teacher, Mr. Nivens, said there was no evidence anything supernatural had ever happened on the Cape. Anyone who believed stories like that was an idiot.

But 'look at me,' the fog seemed to say, 'look at how powerful I am.'

It was so thick the Interceptor headlights just made a bright, blinding glare in front of the windshield. The lined face of Ray Chilensky, the driving instructor at Police Academy, formed out of the fog, saying, 'Don't be a hero.'

That was Ray's catchphrase.

"Finish your shift alive – that's the top priority."

But there were reports of gunfire in Valkyrie. Boone was out there on his own.

"Officer has depressed his personal alarm," a dispatcher said.

I put my foot down and went up to forty, then sixty.

My car hit something big and spun around. My vision went dark. When the lights came back on, my foot was jammed under the gas pedal. I pulled on it a few times. Then I took a deep breath and heaved. Pain shot up my leg.

It was silent outside, save for warm blood squelching at the bottom of my shoe. The fog was aggressively thick.

A Valkyrie police car lay across the road. Its side had been badly smashed up by my car.

The front windshield had a bullet hole in it. I opened the driver's door and checked inside. Empty. A dribbling, blood trail led to a body spread-eagled on the asphalt.

It was a kind, fifty-three year old Valkyrie detective named Andy Rheinholdz, whose daughter Molly had been a year below me in high school. I checked for a pulse and didn't find one. Whoever murdered Andy hadn't taken any chances. His dark, blue shirt and jacket were punctured by a wound in his upper chest, from the size, possibly by a high-powered rifle. The attacker had battered Andy's face with the rifle butt and shot him between the eyes.

Ann's voice came on my radio.

"What's going on out there?"

"I'm in Valkyrie. Officer down. Andy Rheinholdz has been shot. Twice. He's dead."

"Wait for backup."

I was two blocks from the bank where a teller named Bliss Schneider had reported an armed robbery fifteen minutes earlier. The fog was so bad I hobbled blindly up the road, sweeping my hands in front of me.

The Kommerz bank was the tallest building in Valkyrie. It was an imposing, old, concrete building five or six stories high.

A body lay face down on the sidewalk outside the front door. Turning the head around, I recognized the chipmunk cheeks and curly, white hair of Nelson Ayres, an ex-cop and near-retirement security guard. His legs were splayed out at a strange angle that made me look up.

An ear splitting boom thundered overhead. The shock wave blew me off the sidewalk and back onto the road. It went dark for a second.

My ears rang. Hot blood trickled out of my nose.

Chunks of brick and masonry littered the road, but the building's glass front was unharmed. Then I realized, the explosion came from the roof.

"Wait for backup," a little voice inside my head said. But another, louder, voice pointed out no one else was here.

I pushed the bank's big, entrance door open. Fog doesn't do well in heated buildings, so visibility in the foyer was good. The wooden cashier desks were all unmanned. There were blood spatters on the gray marble floor.

One led to the bank teller who had called the cops. Bliss Schneider sat with her back against a square pillar. She was blonde, in her early thirties. She looked calm. Blood from a shoulder wound had spread across her white blouse.

"Hi, are you hurt?" I asked.

"Winged me."

She raised a protecting hand to reveal a ridge of bloody pulp where a bullet had grazed her collar bone. I took a public, first aid kit hanging from the wall and lay a dressing over it.

"What happened here, Bliss?"

"Shooter. On the roof. He's got a high school teacher I had an appointment with, Elliot Hands. And Angie, another teller. And Deputy Washienko."

A hard jolt of terror passed through me.

"He blew a hole in the roof. There are cash and strongboxes up there."

Wait for other officers. But my husband was up there. This guy was a cop-killer. Help could be minutes away, forever in a situation like this.

Bliss's eyes had closed. I squeezed her hand.

"How do I get to the roof?"

Her eyelids fluttered open.

"Use the stairs. No, wait, he'll see you coming through the roof door. Better use the old fire escape outside."

"Thanks. Stay put."

The old, iron fire escape had little platforms on each of the bank's floors. I tried to keep quiet, but the bolts in the stairs rattled. Each step hurt my foot, making me want to cry out.

On the top balcony, I crawled to a low wall surrounding the roof and peered over. The rooftop was a big square of shingle with a smoking hole at one end.

The fog had cleared a little allowing me to see three kneeling figures beside it.

A shadow appeared from nowhere. I saw a rifle butt. My nose became a flower of agony. My gun clattered over the balcony. A hand grabbed my hair and pulled me over the wall.

The bank robber had a thick mop of hair cut an inch above his ears in pudding-bowl style. There was a small swastika on the bridge of his nose. Dark tattoos covered his neck.

"Welcome to the party, Deputy. My name is Ed Henderson Junior, and I am a soldier on a mission."

He had large biceps. He wore an army-style, bulletproof vest over a bare chest. A silver bullet hung from a chain around his neck. His pants were gray camouflage. A semi-automatic rifle rested on his hip.

"Put your handcuffs on for me will you, sweetheart," he said.

I did as he asked.

"Ed, my name is Cassandra. Let the civilians go. No one else has to get hurt."

"Au contraire, my dear."

He grabbed a handful of my hair and dragged me to the other hostages. They knelt amongst piles of strongboxes, cellophane-wrapped bricks of bank notes and loose jewelry. One must have been Elliott Hands. Tall, in his early twenties, Native American. Beside him, Angela Francis, an ordinarily cheerful bank teller in her late forties, white-faced and terrified. Then Boone, whose head was bowed.

A pile of squat metal containers stood in a semi-circle behind them.

Ed threw me down beside Boone. My husband's eyes were glazed and did not look at me. His breathing was shallow. Urine had puddled on the floor between his knees. Seeing the terror on his face was the biggest shock of the day.

A label on a canister read 'Butane/Propane Extreme Mix.' It was making a hissing sound. There were also bricks of waxy explosive with metal detonators stuck in them.

"Ed, why not take the cash and escape in the fog?" I asked.

He took out a brass pocket watch on a long chain and looked at it.

"Two things you need to know about me, darling. One, I'm not here for the cash. Second, I'm not awfully fond of police officers - especially not cowards like your incontinent colleague over there."

He spat in Boone's direction.

This isn't a robbery, I realized.

"Ed, this will make the national news. You can get all the attention you want without killing anyone."

"My orders are to take out key troublemakers and make a field of bones."

"We're not troublemakers," Elliott said.

There were beads of sweat on the teacher's forehead. Ed shook his head.

"The powers that be told me I can take this money with me. Buy a big house with a new car on the driveway in the next life. And a luxury yacht. But there's a price."

"At least let the women go," Elliott said.

Ed winked at him and wagged his finger.

"A little old-fashioned but I like your spirit. Sorry chief. Blood in, blood out."

Ann Ambrose's amplified voice came up from the street.

"This is the County Sheriff's Office. How can we help you resolve this situation?"

Then Boone jumped up, barged Ed aside and ran across the roof. Ed pointed his rifle and fired. There was a puff of pink blood around Boone's leg, but he got over the wall and fell onto the fire escape.

"What a chicken. Guys like that really boil my piss," Ed said.

Angela Francis stood up. Ed held out his rifle and shot her in the face.

"You people are annoying me, now."

The bank robber consulted his watch and looked at the butane canisters.

"Now for the grand finale."

Ed sparked up a metal, wind-proof lighter. I figured we were pretty much dead anyway, so I launched myself forward and grabbed one of his ankles with my handcuffed hands. He fell forward. Elliot crawled over and sat on top of him.

But the bank robber rolled free and got up. He laughed delightedly, holding his lighter in the air, dancing a little jig. Then he tossed it. It fell by the metal containers and lit the pooled gas from a venting canister.

In that last split-second, I felt Elliot try to shield me with his body.

The leaking vessel made an angry whistling sound and blew us both off the roof.

We actually went up at first. The bank roof below was a vast rolling sea of fire. A whole hot universe with its own history and rules.

Up in the air, I remembered how two days earlier I tested positive with a pregnancy kit.

Then I saw something emerge from the thick, black smoke above the flames. It was formed from weasel fog, but human-shaped. It floated on its back. It didn't propel itself. It drifted, like a strong riptide pulled it, but in the air.

The figure reached out. I felt soft arms close around us.

Then we were high above Valkyrie looking down onto Lake Slaughter and the forest canopy of the state park. The Cape looked different – less tended, the trees more gnarled. There were stone structures I had never seen before. With gates in them.

We swooped down towards Franklin Street. Then the arms let go, and we hit the sidewalk, hard.

Chapter Two
Woke

My eyes opened. My husband sat on a chair, reading a newspaper. I was in a hospital bed. My foot was bandaged.

"A Valkyrie cop found you on the sidewalk," Boone said, looking up.

He didn't seem particularly pleased I was awake.

"What happened to Elliott?"

"Who?"

"The other hostage."

"Him? He's fine. He was lying right beside you, safe and sound on the sidewalk."

"How did we survive the fall?"

"Fall? You can't fall off a five-story roof and survive, Cass. There was no fall. You both high-tailed it down the fire escape and left me on the roof to deal with Henderson, remember?"

"What? No. That's not what happened. You ran."

Boone's fists bunched up.

"Wrong, Cass. After you and Elliott fled the scene, the shooter murdered Angela, and I fought him. Harder than I ever fought with anybody in my life. He shot me in the leg. I got to the fire escape before it blew. It was a miracle."

I tried to move. A shooting pain went up my right leg.

"They're going to give me a medal," he said.

His eyes were moist.

"What are you talking about?" I asked.

I tried to sit up. Pain shot up my leg.

"Why is my foot so painful?"

"It was crushed. You lost a toe when you crashed into Andy Rheinholdz' car."

"What about our baby?" I said.

He shook his head.

"Don't go telling any lies to anyone about how I was up there. Your colleagues in the Sheriff's Office don't take kindly to officers who flee and then lie about it."

Boone stood up. I felt light-headed. I remembered my grandma talking to me about telling the truth. About getting lost.

"A man, made out of the fog, held me in his arms," I said.

Boone put his hat on.

"I've got to go to work. Sheriff Fairhurst is coming; you might want to think up a better story. You're delusional. Hysterical. See a psychiatrist."

Hilary 'Hilly' Fairhurst dropped by later. He was a pink-cheeked man with a silver beard who looked like a mid-career Kenny Rogers. The office of Sheriff in Venice County was elected so he was usually all smiles. The look of distaste on his face will haunt me forever.

"An officer fleeing the scene of a crime isn't good for public relations, Deputy."

"I didn't run, sir."

"Folks are keen to hush it up, so you may well get away scot-free. I hear you're Cape."

"I am."

"Shame," he said, and walked out.

The medical staff didn't talk to me. I could see in their eyes they thought I was a coward.

I got angry. I refused to change my story. They moved me to a psychiatric ward. Boone didn't visit. For days I lay on a hospital bed thinking of my lost child. The walls were blank except for a framed poster of a sun-kissed balcony overlooking a calm Mediterranean sea. So unlike my stretch of ocean.

Despair was a river of mud washing through me.

There was a square window in my door. I soon learned that, behind these portholes, people fought heroic, unrecorded struggles.

The hospital was a warren of walkways that looked like actual paths, but in reality, lead nowhere. They were like airport runways where you couldn't take off. A nineteenth century entrepreneur called Julius Wessendorf had built the Lake Slaughter psychiatric hospital. A bronze likeness of him, standing in an inappropriately shrine-like alcove in the hospital chapel, commemorated the pioneer who found the Cape a rock and left it with jobs and prosperity for all.

During the day, people wandered around like they were already ghosts. The nurses only paid attention when someone caused trouble. Not that it mattered. Not that anything mattered.

Days passed. Life came back into focus.

One afternoon, I lay on my bed listening to the radio. There was a knock on the door.

"Anyone home?"

Alphonse Randall walked in. Al was a tall, black man with spiky, orange-colored hair who once flew F15 jets for his country. There was a mass of fire-damaged scar tissue on the left side of his face.

"I bought you a soda from the machine. I should warn you it has a lot of sugar in it."

He sat down on the end of my bed and offered a can of cool, lemon-flavored liquid from the plastic bag that habitually hung from his wrist.

Captain Al Randall had been fighting Gulf War Syndrome for decades. Doctors claimed his pain was psychological.

"Which," Al told me. "Is convenient for insurance people who fob you off with cheap, ineffective mental health treatments."

Ironically, the lack of proper treatment had made him depressed.

"I've been battling demons all weekend," he said.

"Haven't we all?"

"No, actual demons. Y'know, spirits from the next world? There's a lot of that stuff around here, on the Cape, I mean."

"Al, no disrespect, but demons don't exist. Doctor Alvarez would diagnose them as hallucinations," I said.

Al laughed.

"You need to be more open-minded, Cassandra. Folks don't fly in and rescue cops from burning roofs either."

We sipped our sodas for a while.

"For a few days, I've had a feeling a person was watching me; a shadow in the corner of my eye," he said. "A few times, someone has tapped on my observation window. I see a face but, when I open my door, the corridor is empty. I saw a person, last night, standing at the end of my bed - as clear as I see you now."

This story marked a deterioration in Al's health, I thought. I'd had conversations like this with other patients. It's best to listen silently.

"Not demons," Al said. "Maybe that's the wrong word. Ghosts. Dead, anyway. From the Otherworld, off the Cape Misfortune coast."

"I grew up around here, Al. That's folklore."

"Absence of evidence is not evidence of absence. Just because you haven't seen it doesn't mean it isn't real."

He tapped his toe on the floor and winked.

"What does your doctor say?"

"I'm not fond of my new shrink. Her name is Dame Teddy Champion. The Dame is because she is British, from London. My new contacts in the spirit world tell me she may soon become the senior consultant here."

We sipped our sodas.

"She put a rent-a-cop on the front door of the hospital. His name is Rieper - everyone calls him the "Grim Rieper". He has two holsters for a gun and a Taser. Dresses like he's in Special Forces. Something bad is brewing. I'm getting out of the Cape. Heading out for the territories, maybe even tonight."

My door burst open to reveal our Senior Staff Nurse, Trudy Hopkins. Her blonde hair was tied up in a glossy bun. She had a wide mouth and wore lots of makeup. Nurse Hopkins saw patients as a hated obstacle to her ward running smoothly.

"You're not allowed in each other's rooms. You can associate in the lounge. You know the rules. Out."

She jerked her thumb towards the corridor.

"Excuse me. We're having a conversation," Al said. "We're not five years old."

Al sipped his soda. Hopkins pressed the red button on a key fob hanging from her belt. A piercing alarm sounded in the air.

Within seconds my room filled with a dozen nurses and orderlies. Nurse Paul Rowlands, a blonde-haired man in his early thirties who acted as Hopkins' chief enabler, stood at the front, hands on hips. The snaking veins in his forearms were popping up. Rowlands learned restraint techniques in college and consequently thought he was a tough guy.

"Al, let's go to the lounge," I said.

"These patients were engaged in inappropriate behavior. They became abusive when asked to stop," Hopkins said.

"That's bullshit," Al said.

"Watch your language," Rowlands said.

Al sipped his soda. He looked calm, but his hand was shaking.

"Hopkins, you're in the pay of Dame Teddy and the bad guys. I know that now."

Rowlands twisted Al's arm behind his back and pushed him into a standing position.

"Using abusive language to a nurse."

"That's a lie," I said.

"You watch your mouth as well," Rowlands said, manhandling Al out of the door.

I really need to leave here, I thought.

Later that day, I saw an unlikely face in my door's little, glass window. Boone. He had hardly visited. His handsome features attempted sympathy but there was a hint of, "I'm suffering too - maybe more than you are."

"How are you doing?"

"Considering I'm in the nuthouse, okay."

"I've been thinking."

"Boone."

"Let me speak."

"Please," I said. "Don't start a fight. Not in here."

"I think we should separate."

"Is this because of what happened on the roof?"

His eyes widened with anger.

"It has nothing to do with that."

"I changed my story. I said what they…you…want me to say."

"Stop talking about that. The Sheriff's Office wants that whole thing covered up now. This is about us. This will be better for both of us."

I started to cry. I didn't want to.

"How is this better for me?"

Imagining a future without Boone was like imagining the world without the sun.

"We've been tearing each other apart."

"I've been ill."

"I'm not a saint, Cass. I don't like coming to places like this."

He looked around my room.

"I'd prefer it if you didn't call me for a while. I find it too upsetting. Maybe send a text, or an email, if you have to. But not while I'm on duty."

"Boone."

He walked to the door, stopped, and turned.

"I'd like my grandma's wedding ring back."

I looked at the gold band on my finger.

Boone held out his hand. He didn't look at me directly. It felt like I was watching someone else. Another couple.

Later that night, I played a melancholy playlist on my phone and turned the volume up. I smashed a porcelain mug and used a jagged shard to saw into my wrist. I lay on the floor. Blood pooled beside me. I thought of the ocean I wouldn't see again.

Then I dreamt I was in a much, much bigger hospital. As big as a city. Weeds and creepers curled around rows of rusty beds. A gust of bitter wind rattled the window frames. A flurry of snow fell through a broken skylight. Someone stirred in the bed next to mine. My sister, Agata. Her face was thin and pale.

An alarm went off. I was wheeled to the Emergency Room in the real hospital. A disapproving young doctor sewed me up.

In the morning, Hopkins stood by the end of my bed.

"The cleaner found pieces of broken cup on the floor. She could have cut her finger off."

"I'm sorry."

"Selfish," she said. "Lockdown until further notice."

As I fell asleep, I recollected the figure emerging out of the fog. Clearly remembered it.

I sat up. Nurse Rowlands was asleep in an armchair outside my half-open door. His job was to closely observe me all night but, as usual, he had nodded off shortly after the corridor lights were dimmed.

My window was locked and looked out onto a fence. Tonight, rain drummed against it. At first, it sounded like someone gargling water. Then the noise formed into a sequence of notes; a sad melody I knew from somewhere.

A circle on the wall, beside my bed, wobbled. It came alive, melting into rippling liquid. A small hole in its center wept drops of brown ooze that smelt like rotten meat.

The strange melancholy notes became words.

"Who will be my number six?" they asked.

I recognized the voice.

"You only killed four innocent people. Andy Rheinholdz, Ayres, Angela Francis - and your wife, Joanne, half an hour before you blew yourself up on the roof."

Something stood at the end of my bed. The bullet necklace hung around a non-existent neck. There was no body, just the glowing orange outlines of his many prison tattoos. They filled the room with a dim light.

"Why d'you kill all those people anyway?" I said.

His voice wasn't rainfall anymore.

"It was a test. See if I was a team player. They were casualties of war, darling. I'm a soldier. Special Forces. Behind enemy lines."

"You're dead, Ed."

"Yet here I am talking to you, Deputy Dipshit."

"So, where do scumbags go when they die, Ed?"

"You'll find out soon enough."

"I'm hallucinating. New meds."

Ed chuckled.

"Dr. Alvarez got you drugged up, has he? He should try the new talking therapies. They worked with me."

"You don't exist," I said.

His tattoos flared. A finger tweaked my non-existent toe.

"I need you to do something difficult for me, darling. An execution. Take a life to save a life."

"What?"

Nurse Rowlands muttered something and scratched his nose. Ed pointed at him with a glowing finger.

"This fella is on the way to being a top nurse. Does what he's told. Be like him. Soon you could be driving your sissy, cop car with the whirly lights."

I sat up on my bed and reached out until my fingers brushed his pectoral tattoos - a grim reaper and a clock with no hands. They felt cold, then my hand passed straight through.

"Just out of interest, what do you want me to do?"

"Kill the chief headshrinker here, Dr. Joachim Alvarez."

I laughed.

"I'd get life in the state funny farm."

"Not if you do it right. You're a resourceful young woman."

"What's Alvarez done to you?"

"It isn't me, darling. Personally, I don't care. If it were up to me, I'd kill you now," Ed said. "Hang you from a rail in the closet like an old fur coat. Leave a realistic suicide note, Cape Misfortune style.

"This isn't happening."

"Oh, it is. It's orders. The new girl, Dame Teddy Champion, has big plans for this place."

"You can forget it. I'm not going to do anything for you."

"Things will go easier for you, and your mom if you do what you're told."

"My mom?"

"Oh, didn't I say? She dies if you don't help. That's the life you're saving."

The flickering figure spat. A ghostly gob hit the floor and exploded in a puff of luminous smoke. Then he was gone. A single flake of black ash fell onto my blanket.

Rowlands was fast asleep.

I got up and carefully unclipped the keys hanging from a lanyard on his belt. I then tiptoed up the linoleum corridor. The side windows looked out onto an expanse of rolling, soulless turf outside the hospital.

There was no one at the nurse's station. I unlocked the door to the ward's little store room. There was a row of cell phones charging on a table. I picked mine out.

My Mom kept a landline telephone on a bedside cabinet. She always picked it up. Tonight, it rang and rang. I phoned my ex-husband.

"Boone?"

"No phone calls."

"My mom isn't answering her phone."

"So? Maybe she's out."

"She's never out."

"You try her cell?"

"She doesn't have one."

"What do you want me to do?"

"Get a Venice cop to knock on the door."

"Dial 911 if you're that worried."

"Boone, my phone says there is a forecast for fog. The Weasel, probably."

He hesitated.

"So?"

"Can you drop by her house before it arrives? Please. It's a couple of minutes away."

"Okay. But you need to respect my boundaries and not phone me. You're not the only one suffering here."

He phoned back a few minutes later.

"I found a possible sign of forced entry."

"What?"

"One of the windows on the back door is broken."

"Can you go in?"

"I'm going to call this in."

"Go in now. My mom's life is in danger."

When I turned Rowlands stood in the doorway.

"I'm having a family emergency. I have to leave," I said.

Rowlands shook his head.

"No can do, Cassandra."

"I'll report you for being asleep," I said.

He thought for a second then smiled.

"I wasn't."

I barged past him and ran into one of the patient gardens, a paved area with weedy flower beds and piles of cigarette butts.

The ward alarm sounded. Margaret, a homely sixty year old who advised tea drinking as the cure for any crisis, crushed a cigarette under her heel.

"I'm leaving," I said.

She shook her head.

"Not without seeing a doctor first."

There was a wooden fence around the garden. I climbed up. Margaret grabbed my legs. My bare heel connected with the top of her head and I pushed myself over, falling onto turf on the other side.

It was the first time I had seen the hospital at night. It looked better on the outside – graceful, brick and stone buildings with turrets lining the roof. It had a clock tower. Rowlands ran out of the front doors. The new rent-a-cop, 'Grim' Rieper, followed behind. He had the look of a bodybuilder. His hair had a samurai-style top-knot. He wore a bulletproof vest and two holsters, one held a Taser and the other a pistol.

I ran through the parking lot.

I felt a sharp sting in my back. I learned to Taser at the academy, but not on the receiving end. It felt like every muscle in my body was electrocuted. My body collapsed under me. When the electricity stopped, I felt a knee in the small of my back. A bunch of people piled on top of me. Someone stuck a syringe into my backside.

My body stopped responding to my brain. I lay with my face against asphalt, dribbling from the side of my mouth. Al had warned me about Vacuphase. An emergency therapy of last-resort to disable violent patients.

Two orderlies carried me back on a stretcher and dumped me on a bed in intensive care. In the dark room, glowing tattoos cast a dim, malevolent light over the walls.

Ed Henderson chuckled.

"Well, that was a screw up. You're no good to us in your current, vegetable state. On the upside, I may finally be allowed to kill you."

I tried to speak, but my jaw wouldn't obey my brain.

In the morning, the door to the ICU opened and Doctor Joachim Alvarez walked in, followed by Nurse Hopkins, who carried a clipboard.

"How are you feeling, Cassandra?"

My vision was blurred, but I made out his plump face and horn-rimmed glasses.

"Not a huge fan of Vacuphase," I croaked.

He grimaced.

"Wouldn't have been my first choice. The drug will wear off in another twelve to forty-eight hours. Tell me, why did you try to leave us last night?"

"My mom was in danger."

"Really. How did you know that?"

"I tried to phone her. She didn't answer. She always answers."

Alvarez stroked his chin.

"How did you phone her?"

"On my cell."

"Cassandra, when you were admitted do you remember they took away your charging cord - as they do with anyone who is considered a danger to themselves? Your phone has been dead for days.

He held my phone up to me. The screen was dead.

"Nurse Hopkins phoned your mother this morning. She was absolutely fine."

"There was a break in. I spoke to my husband."

"I just got off the phone with Deputy Washienko. He hadn't heard from you either," Hopkins said.

"When people become acutely ill, they may hear or see things that aren't real," Alvarez said.

"You're in danger," I said.

Alvarez sighed.

"I don't think we're making progress. In fact, just the opposite. The patient is proving resistant to treatment. We need to try new therapies. Have you heard of electroconvulsive therapy?"

"I saw someone last night who told me you are in danger," I said.

"Who told you?"

"Ed Henderson."

"The dead bank robber?"

"Yes. He told me to kill you."

Alvarez was quiet for a second. He looked at Hopkins, who shrugged.

"Why?"

"Dame Teddy Champion wants your job."

The doctor laughed.

"That may well be true. But that's something for me to worry about."

He squeezed my shoulder.

"Take it easy, Cassie."

"That won't be a problem. I can't move."

The ICU door swung open, and Al Randall walked in. There was a film of sweat on his fire-damaged face.

"You're not allowed in here," Hopkins said.

"So sorry," Al said. "I have no choice."

He searched in his plastic bag and took out a long shard of glass. It had a handle made of masking tape.

"He said they would hurt my kids."

"Wait. Who did?"

"The dead bank robber, Ed Henderson. They sent me a photo. My wife phoned me a few minutes later. Said she and the girls had been taken."

Al held his cell phone up. The screen was dead.

"Al, they took the cord off you, remember?" I reminded him.

Al looked at the phone and frowned.

"Oh yeah," he said.

He dropped his homemade dagger onto the floor.

Hopkins hit the alarm on the wall.

A second later Karl Rieper ran in, pistol already drawn.

Alvarez moved into my line of sight, so I couldn't see anything.

"The situation's under control, Karl," I heard him say. "There's no need for that now."

A gun fired. Someone fell to the floor.

"Have you lost your mind?" Alvarez said.

There was no answer. Then the doctor grunted with pain. I saw Al's homemade shank pierce his neck in vicious, rapid stabs. Dr. Alvarez fell on me.

There was silence. I could smell his blood. It trickled down my cheek.

He turned his head to me. He whispered something, but I couldn't hear him clearly.

It sounded like, "Sorry."

"Hang in there," I said.

A bunch of Valkyrie cops and medics arrived ten minutes later. I knew most of them. It was too late for my consultant psychiatrist, who had long-since stopped breathing.

When the Vacuphase wore off, Hopkins wheeled me back to the ward.

"I always knew Al Randall was bad news," she said.

In the evening, a Valkyrie detective called Ulrich Honeyglass walked into my room. He was a wiry man, in his early fifties, who was a golfing buddy of Police Captain Hank Frederson and had a permanent poker face. He took out a notebook.

"So, the hero of the hour, Karl Rieper, hears a commotion, rushes in, sees Al Randall shanking the doc - and shoots him."

"The gun went off before the stabbing."

Honeyglass frowned.

"That doesn't make any sense."

"It's what happened."

"The doc fell on you. You couldn't see anything."

"I heard a shot. Someone, probably Captain Randall, fell to the floor. Dr. Alvarez was knifed after that.

"By who?"

"I couldn't see. Someone in the room."

The detective snapped his notebook shut.

"We already have statements from reliable witnesses. I'm sure data from the crime scene will corroborate their story."

"I'm sure it will, too."

He looked around to check no one was in earshot.

"Karl Rieper saved your life from that nut job. He's the kind of guy who runs towards crime scenes, not away from them."

I asked to see a psychiatrist about leaving the hospital. A week later I went for a consultation in the late Dr. Alvarez's office. On my last visit to Joachim's room, the decor had been bare and the surfaces piled high with old files. Now bookcases lined each wall, filled with medical journals bound in gilt-edged binders.

The woman behind a new, oversized desk looked small and athletic. She wore a two-piece, grey, felt dress. Her hair was jet black. Her smooth, uniformly pink skin made guessing an age difficult. She gestured to a seat.

"I'm your new consultant. Dame Teddy Champion. How are you diddling, my dear? Things have been frightfully eventful. Your friend Al proved quite handy with that shank."

She picked up a silver letter opener and mimed a few stabs. Then she laughed.

"I want to discharge myself," I said.

Dame Teddy raised her eyebrows.

"Do you indeed?"

"I'm here voluntarily. I feel better."

"I'll be the judge of that. How well did you know the murderer, Al Randall?"

"Captain Randall was a good guy."

"Were you in cahoots with him?"

"What?"

Her eyes widened.

"The good Nurse Hopkins has got me up to speed about his frequent visits to your room. Did you have inappropriate feelings for the dashing, battle-scarred Captain?"

"He was a friend."

"Were you lovers?"

"No. He was married."

"Ah, but the good ones always are, isn't that the old saying?"

She walked around her desk until we were a few inches apart. She held out her hands and brushed the tips of her fingers on the nape of my neck.

"Tell me, did you plot poor Joachim Alvarez's death with your lover, Al Randall?"

I knocked her hands away.

"Absolutely not. This is totally inappropriate."

Dame Teddy licked her lips and wandered over to a window that overlooked a distant Lake Slaughter.

"There's too much failure on this stupid rock. Cape Misfortune is such a dreary name. I'm going to get the name changed. I have wonderful friends on the Venice City council."

"I'm discharging myself."

"Did you know Randall was going to murder my dear friend, Joachim Alvarez?"

"I don't think he killed Dr. Alvarez," I said.

Dame Teddy raised an eyebrow.

"What a silly story. Young Karl Rieper is one of my most precious favorites. Anyway, who will believe the opinion of a madwoman who saw a flying man on a rooftop?"

"Mad is an old-fashioned word for a psychiatrist to use."

"It's just shorthand," she said, waving her hand dismissively. "You shouldn't be so politically correct."

"Let me go."

"I can do more than that."

She stuck her tongue out and touched the tip of her nose.

"If you want to get back to the Sheriff's Office, you need to work with me, Cassandra. You cooperate with old Aunty Teddy and she'll get you a golden ticket out of this giggling academy. Back in your pretty uniform, with a pop-gun and big car. I'm a friend of Captain Hank Frederson. A very close friend."

Something broke in me. The reality of my situation overwhelmed me.

"I've already said I imagined the figure in the fog," I said.

She wagged a finger.

"Do you think wicked old Teddy plotted to kill boring old Doctor Alvarez?"

I shook my head.

"No."

"Then who killed my predecessor?"

"I couldn't see."

Teddy clapped her hands together.

"Oh, sweetheart. Now doesn't that just put the flower in my button hole?"

Chapter Three
The Return of Cassandra Dollar

I have always loved to visit the strange borderlands where ocean meets shore. When half my family disappeared, swimming gave me structure. Once again, it was my way back.

The advice in Cape Misfortune is not to swim.

Bridging the join between land and sea is perilous here. Rocks and driftwood hide in the roaring breakers. The water is always chilly. A cold current flows down from Alaska. If you insist on getting in, try a wetsuit unless you want a permanent, ice-cream headache all over your body.

What do they usually call it when you first immerse yourself in water - an embrace? Not here. Intimate, certainly, but also cruel, like close combat.

Beyond the surf, sinkholes appear from nowhere to snare you, even a few feet from the shore. The beaches are steep on this side of America, so you're always near deep water.

But you can drift now, your body tiny and buoyant in an immensity of molten light. Stay vigilant, though. Keep your distance from the shore. The sea can break a body's bones on the rocks.

Watch out for riptides. If you see plastic bottles or detergent foam floating out to sea, chances are you've found one. That, or a channel of dark, choppy water. Who knows where those deadly tides end up? Grandma claimed they swept the unwary to beaches on dark islands across the sea.

Why do I do it? I can't say I love the water. It's why I stayed on this coast when I should have traveled a thousand miles away.

I told Dame Teddy that Ed Henderson was a hallucination. I said there was no flying man. I told the cops Boone didn't wet himself or flee the scene. I got back to Ulrich Honeyglass. I said I wasn't sure about the events in the ICU.

Grandma warned us about telling lies but I wasn't going to be written off as a Cape crazy. I wanted a life. So, I collaborated.

Teddy discharged me. She walked around the desk, put her hands on my shoulders.

"I don't think you're a danger to others, darling, or to yourself. I think you're dangerously cute."

"I'm feeling better now," I said.

"We have to play with the cards we are dealt, dear girl. Don't expect happiness today. But, if you are good, it may come tomorrow."

I read about a tribe who believed humans know everything when they are born but forget it as adults. I hoped this period of pain would be like that. In time, I would forget all this terrible knowledge. Each night I set aside time to cry, scheduled it right in.

When I reported for work in the little substation, someone had cleared the pictures and belongings off my desk. Ann Ambrose didn't look up from her paperwork.

"Good morning, ma'am," I said.

She took a good couple of minutes to finish writing something.

"I was told last week that the psychiatric evaluation gave you a clean bill of health," she said. "Captain Frederson phoned me up personally to say you are re-joining the team. That's the first time that Handsome Hank has spoken to me in thirteen years. I'll tell you the same thing I told him. I don't think you should come back."

"I'm ready to be here, ma'am."

"Are you certain you still want to be a police officer? Is there anything I can do to change your mind?"

"No."

"The Sheriff's Office runs the County jail. They're short of correctional officers. I'd put in a good word for you."

"I want to be here."

"With a health record like yours, you are lucky to be still wearing that uniform."

"Yes, ma'am."

"It's nothing personal but I think you will be a danger to whoever you go out with."

"I hope that's not the case, ma'am."

"Your own husband stood where you are now and told me you ran from an active crime scene."

"Ex-husband."

"Female officers are thin on the ground around here. We need ambassadors. You let the side down. I've heard of people freezing up before. I've seen it. But fleeing the scene? Some people just aren't cut out for this job."

"I hope I can prove you wrong."

"I'm not even sure if it's safe to send you out to patrol on your own. But, unfortunately, we don't have the manpower to babysit cowards."

The last word hung in the air.

"May I go on patrol?" I asked.

She stared at me for a few seconds. Then she took the car keys out of her desk drawer and threw them at me.

I walked outside and took a deep breath.

Sometimes, we have to reconcile ourselves to a new reality. But keeping quiet about the events on the bank roof was like burning coal in my brain.

It started raining. I drove across Cape Misfortune's salt marshes, surprised to be behind the wheel again.

I returned to the drunk drivers, shoplifters, stray animals and domestic abusers of the Cape. Then I did it all again the next day. And the next, usually with the same perpetrators.

None of the other cops spoke to me. Ann was itching to get rid of me. I kept my nose clean.

I bought our old farm back.

I drove past one afternoon and found it was up for sale. Accountants representing the developer, now bankrupt, were selling a bunch of old properties.

A sympathetic real estate agent called Sandy, whom I knew from school, told me to hurry because the Coffi Corporation was buying everything.

I phoned my mother.

"Why on earth would you want to move back there, Cassie?"

"I don't know."

"It's cursed. Aggie went missing from there."

"Aggie loved the farm. So did Dad. So did you, once. I'm not asking you to live there with me, Mom."

"It's derelict."

"I know things haven't been great with us. I've never asked you for anything before. You'll get it back."

"Do you want to buy the land as well?"

"Yes, all of it."

"Why? Farming equipment is so expensive."

"That'll come later."

"I'll help you," she said. "But I can't visit."

Sandy was a Goth with a pierced nose who wore a pinstripe suit. I met her on a sunny Saturday morning.

She was not a fan of Coffi buying up the Cape properties.

"This rock used to be a nice place to live," she said.

We walked up the path I knew so well, barely visible amongst the flourishing wildflowers, to the Prize.

The old homestead wasn't much to look at, now – just a half-ruined two-story shack. The rotten wood and flaking paint looked even worse than when I stayed here illegally. But she was a friend I had thought was lost forever.

We stopped at the front porch. I looked up at the little verandah above the front door where Aggie and I had sometimes read books.

The door below was boarded up.

"You can't live here until it's legally habitable," Sandy said.

"Okay."

She smiled.

"I grew up on a farm just up the coast. Prices have gone down because of the planned pipeline but I wouldn't be surprised if Coffi phone you pretty soon and offer triple what you paid for it. You could make a fast buck. But I don't think you're interested in that."

She hugged me.

"Good luck."

A wooden chest on the back porch still held my parents' old tent. Miraculously, the canvas had not perished. I set it up on the meadow behind the house.

That night I watched the sun set on a wild garden.

All the land, my land, bent to the ocean. I watched the water's ever-changing patterns of light.

It was a few weeks before spring and the coast bats were waking from hibernation to rear their new pups. They thronged in the air, dive-bombing the bogs for a meal.

When it got dark, I lay down in the tent. I heard the familiar sound of the far off surf. It started raining.

Then I saw a shadow on the canvas.

"I'm armed," I said.

"I'm not," said a voice outside.

I opened the flap and stuck my head out. It was Elliott Hands, my fellow rooftop survivor. He was wearing volunteer Coast Guard overalls. His expression, lit by my flashlight, was a little haunted.

"How do you know I live here?" I said.

"I saw you in town and followed you."

"Well, that's honest, at least. Stalking as well as trespass."

"Maybe wait to hear what I've come to say first."

"Wait while I put some clothes on."

Elliott sat on my grandma's porch steps, head in hands, black hair spilling through his fingers.

"Do you want some hot tea?" I asked. "I have a gas cooker."

He shook his head.

"I came here because I saw a figure in the fog on the roof."

That stopped me in my tracks.

"Why didn't you say anything?"

"Why didn't you?"

"I did. They locked me up in the funny farm."

Elliott smiled. I liked it. I sat down beside him. We stared out at the oversized weeds in the derelict bogs.

"Displaced Indians came back to work on the fields around here...before harvesting machines. Hard work for not a lot of pay."

"My parents didn't get here until the late 1990s."

"I don't think it's very safe for you out here," Elliott said. "It's isolated."

"You think I'm in danger?"

"Maybe. I wasn't in the bank by chance that morning. I had an appointment with Bliss Schneider about a loan."

"So?"

"She was nervous and distracted when I arrived."

"This was before the shooter turned up?"

"Right. When Henderson came into the bank, before anyone knew what was in his sports bag, he looked at Schneider. Their eyes met for a second. There was recognition. They knew each other. That was my instinct."

"He shot her."

"She screwed up her eyes, but a second too early, like it was rehearsed."

"Which was also not in your statement."

"I've hardly slept since it happened."

He got up and stood in front of me.

"What if it all was connected?"

"What?"

"All of it. I helped organize a protest committee about the new pipeline. You know who else was on it? Ayres, the security guard. Angela, the teller, ran a blog criticizing the Coffi Corporation."

"I remember. 'Wake Up and Smell the Coffi,'"

"What if this wasn't a bank robbery or a crazed shooter, but a way of executing troublemakers?"

The rain got harder. Two separate streams of rainwater were now leaking through the porch roof.

"The FBI and state police checked Henderson's background," I said. "He was a lone wolf."

"Did you know the Detective who was shot, Rheinholdz?"

"Sure, I worked with him. He was in the wrong place at the wrong time."

"What if he was on the list? What if you were on it? Just thinking out loud, here," Elliott said.

I shook my head.

"That would take a lot of organization. They would have needed to know the duty rotation for Rheinholdz and me. And Ayres too, if you think about it. I swapped at the last minute. I took Dan Ridley's day. It's a coincidence."

"But what if it wasn't? We saw the figure in the fog. We were rescued. We should be dead. Something's going on."

"You should have spoken up at the time, Elliott."

He sighed.

"Yeah, I should have. Could you at least look into Bliss Schneider?"

I shook my head.

"I'd lose my job. Bliss is a hero. She stayed to call the cops."

Elliott shivered.

"Looks like I made a mistake coming here," he said.

"You want some free advice - stay away from Bliss."

He walked off into the rain.

I sat for a while. I was glad he had seen the fog man, and I wanted to help him - but I couldn't.

Chapter Four
Vincent

A week after my return to keeping the peace, I drove a middle-aged heroin addict across overcast, salt marshes. The Sheriffs' Association had recently downgraded drug possession to a misdemeanor. We now drove addicts to a charity-run rehab on the fringes of the state park rather than the county jail.

I picked Vincent Deary up from the Valkyrie cells where he was being held for stealing two hundred bucks from his elderly mother. He was pitifully thin and his clothes were stained with dirt. A cop had found him collapsed on a beach.

As we drove, he leaned forward in his seat and spoke through the mesh.

"They're running Cape Misfortune into the ground. Bad things are going on here."

"Like what, Vincent?"

"You be careful, Deputy. This rock is no place for honest people."

"Tell me about it," I said.

Farson rehab was an unassuming brick building in a copse of tall pines. Once I had signed all the paperwork, Vincent shook my hand.

That, I hoped, was that.

Next day, towards the end of my shift, dispatch gave the code for aggravated burglary at an address in Wish Bay. The new Wessendorf house, I thought.

"En route," I said.

The estate stood on top of a rocky hill. The big house was square, made of yellow sandstone with medieval-style towers on each corner. It was backed by a lawn that sloped down to the cliffs.

There was a stone wall around the grounds, but the front gate was open. A banner above it said, 'Elect Police Captain 'Handsome' Hank Frederson for Sheriff.' There was a picture of a tanned, square-jawed man with sparkling blue eyes and a cheesy grin.

I parked beside a tennis court and stood by my car. After what happened at the bank, I was careful to wait for other officers.

Then I heard gunfire in the building. After an internal debate that lasted two seconds, I ran over a gravel drive towards a wooden barn to the left of the house. Light spilled out from a central door.

I looked in and saw a cavernous room with a polished, wooden floor. Three figures stood over a body.

"Police, put your hands up," I ordered.

"Take it easy, Deputy," a deep, growling voice said.

"Sir, drop your weapon."

A tall figure placed a gun on the floor.

'Handsome Hank' had a mahogany tan and looked a lot younger than his sixty years. Tonight, he was dressed in a tailored, white tuxedo. He did not give me his famous toothy grin. Beside him, a small woman in a ball gown toasted me with a glass of champagne. My shrink, Dame Teddy. Next to her Karl 'Grim' Rieper watched me.

Vincent Deary lay at their feet. The back of his head was a cratered pulp. Blood and brains were sprayed across the floor. He held a small pistol in his right hand.

I felt his pulse.

"Dead."

"As a door nail," Teddy said.

"A bullet to the head can do that," Hank said.

"Who shot him?"

"Me," Hank replied, picking up the long-barreled Sig Hauer pistol he had placed on the floor.

"Our Sheriff-to-be is a genuine hero," Dame Teddy said, squeezing his biceps.

"Where's your holster, Captain?" I said.

"He keeps the gun in the back waistband of my pants," Teddy said. "Otherwise it affects the line of his tux."

"You always carry a high-caliber handgun there when you're off-duty?" I asked.

Hank nodded.

"I do. Otherwise, I would be dead now."

"This man's name was Vincent Deary," I said. "He was a substance-abuser I dropped off in rehab recently."

"Rehab? He just tried to murder a police captain. This is exactly why we need a new sheriff," said Frederson.

"He had no history of violence."

I looked at Rieper.

"You carrying a concealed weapon?"

"Not even my Taser."

He smiled the ghost of a smile.

"Did Deary say what he wanted?" I said, turning to Hank.

Hank shook his head.

"He was a junkie trying to rob rich people, and he got shot, as any half-decent cop would realize."

"Cassandra is one of our brightest young deputies," Teddy said.

"I only heard one shot. Did Deary discharge his weapon?" I said.

"No," Hank said. "He ran in waving his gun around. I didn't stop to ask questions."

"Anyone else see Deary's gun?"

"I did," Rieper said.

"So did I," Teddy said.

I looked around the empty room.

"Where are the other guests?"

"Not due for fifteen minutes," Teddy said. "Now, if you don't mind, I think we should carry on with the fundraiser. That will show handsome Hank Frederson is the hero of the bulldog breed."

It looked like she squeezed Hank's backside.

"This is a crime scene," I said.

"We will find another room. Bear & Hart Wessendorf may come down from their towers. Maybe old Pop, himself."

"The show must go on," Frederson said, as he ran a hand through his hair.

"This disturbed young man may just have won us the election," Teddy said. "It will read well on the front page of the *Cape Misfortune Sentinel*."

I had a hunch that Rieper pulled the trigger, not Hank.

Boone and a few other cops turned up. None of them spoke to me.

Chapter Five
Shorebird

That night, I dream I am a shorebird flying high over the Misfortune coast, riding the winds, crisscrossing the border between the dark cliffs and massing ocean.

Basket traps to catch salmon are set out on the lower reaches of the river, which flows with clear water fed from mountain canyons. There is no Valkyrie town yet. This is another when.

A bunch of gold prospectors, carrying pistols and rifles, make their way towards a native village in a forest clearing.

That particular story doesn't end well. Later, a vulture lies in wait for a wounded infant to die.

The survivors march north on the promise of a reservation that doesn't exist.

I fly along the coast and forward a few years in time to the sacred grandmother rock, sitting at the ocean's mouth, stubbornly blocking big, steam-driven boats from traveling upriver. Men from the Army Corps of Engineers jam fingers in their ears and blow it up.

The shock wave knocks me out of the sky into a cold but beloved Wish Bay. It is our future now, not the past. Beams of light from the morning sun trickle down from the ocean surface on something new.

There is a dark hole in the rocky floor of the bay, so ancient and natural-looking it could have been carved by chance and time. But there are symbols around it that could be an invitation or warning. Things are moving inside. Thousands of shadows. An army is getting ready.

Then the bay is flooded with a fast-moving chemical cloud, dark as night, black ink with a touch like acid.

I fly out of the ocean into the safety of a shore breeze. Someone tumbles around in the air, above Wish Bay, as if caught in a whirling tide. They start circling the sharp peak of Needlepoint rock. I know I have seen it, him, before. The rescuer from the Kommerz bank roof.

The shadow holds out his hand. He touches my head with his forefinger. An arrow of light strikes me.

I woke to the sound of rain pitter-pattering on the canvas.

"Anyone in there?" a voice asked.

I sat up.

"What do you want?"

"We're here to fix the house."

I pulled my uniform shirt on and climbed out. It was raining hard. Two men dressed in plastic ponchos stared at me. The older one had a barrel chest and bushy eyebrows.

"Are you Cassandra Dollar? He asked. "My name is Kurt Deakins. This is my son Francesco."

"I haven't hired anyone."

The younger man had long, red hair and a wispy beard. He dumped an armful of scaffolding rods onto the ground.

"We've been contracted to make this property safe for occupation."

Kurt held out an envelope. I ripped it open. A white card had one word on it, written in my mother's handwriting.

"PLEASE."

"I'm sorry, gents," I said. "I'm going to have to ask you to get off my property."

"I'm a friend of your mom. She never really recovered from your sister and your dad going missing. She knows that. She wants to start making things right between you before it's too late."

"She hates this place," I said. "I asked her to help with a deposit. I can't afford any renovation work.

"She's trying to make things right," Francesco said.

"How much will this cost?" I said.

Kurt Deakin looked over at the house and narrowed his eyes.

"To say it's a fixer-upper is an understatement. It needs to be stripped down to the studs. There's rot in all the wood, and beetle. The roof joists are ready to collapse."

They both stared at me.

"Okay," I said.

Kurt nodded. The two men started putting up scaffolding.

The engine on a beaten up, old, estate car I bought before I got married chose this particular morning to give up the ghost. Francesco gave me a lift to work in his van.

As usual, Ann gave me the silent treatment.

It was a few minutes before my shift officially started. I took the patrol car up to the parking lot on Wish Bay, a square of asphalt on a grassy cliff edge, to watch the sun on the water. The sky was clear. I watched gulls and cormorants ride the air.

One of my earliest memories was my father's brother, Leo, dying down there. We were five. Or six. He was rowing us out to sea.

"Girls, I think I am going to have forty winks," he said, as he clutched his chest.

He slumped backward. We thought it was a joke. Then Aggie handed me an oar. We rowed back. My dead uncle's face was set in the last reassuring smile he had given us in life.

I opened the boxy, souped-up laptop that served as the Interceptor's mobile computer terminal. The machine booted into a screen showing the Venice County Sheriff's star.

I pulled Bliss Schneider's records. Twenty-nine years old. She lived above a convenience store in Valkyrie. A Class B felony for breaking another woman's cheekbone outside a Valkyrie nightclub. No prison time, but sent for a psychiatric evaluation. Psychiatrist: Dame Teddy Champion.

"Of course," I said.

Next, I looked up Elliott. No rap sheet. House on the Western cape coast. Taught social sciences and gym at high school. Volunteer for Cape Misfortune Coast Guard.

His witness statement about the Kommerz bank wasn't long. He claimed he couldn't remember anything.

I closed the computer and looked at Needle Point, encircled in endlessly thrashing surf. A light, morning mist stealing across the water made it look like the ruined gatepost of an ancient fence.

A gust of rain hit the windshield and startled me. Raindrops drummed hard on the glass and formed into sounds. A sad melody.

A shadow flitted across the patrol car's back window. The vehicle started to bounce up and down as if a giant had got hold of the back bumper. Then the car slid down a steep grass verge towards the cliff edge. I fired the engine up and reversed, hard. The wheels skidded as my car battled the invisible attacker. I watched in disbelief as I moved towards my almost-certain death, inch by inch. I took out my pistol and fired at the rear windshield, shattering the glass. The car skidded backward up the grass into the parking lot.

Something ran over the hill. I swung the car around and drove after them. When I got over the brow of the hill, there was no one there.

I got out and stared at the hole in the rear window. No one would believe me. Discharging a weapon without cause could give Ann the excuse she wanted. I took out my baton and smashed the cracked glass out.

I watched the bay for a while, trying to get calm. Elliot would go after Schneider. That was inevitable. It would mean trouble for him.

The car radio came on and reported a disturbance in Valkyrie shipyard.

Most of the state and local police forces were dressed up in riot gear when I got there. I pulled a helmet, bulletproof vest and forearm pads from the car's trunk.

The Wessendorf factory had made ships that sailed across the globe. Julius Wessendorf built what was then the largest, roofed dry dock in the world. My dad said it was so big inside, they used bicycles to get around. The docks employed most of Cape Misfortune. It was building battleships and cruisers right up until the 1970s.

Some of the assembly buildings were derelict now. A few were repurposed. One was a wine warehouse, another a yacht salesroom.

Up ahead, I saw a group of men and women in a muddy courtyard. They had gathered beneath one of the assembly building's five hundred foot high doors.

There were no protest signs. Just bewildered and angry people. Many were middle-aged. Some wore overalls. One wore a business suit.

"Coffi closed it all down at eight-thirty this morning and the natives are getting restless," Detective Ulrich Honeyglass told me, from under his riot helmet. "Heard you were back, don't flake out on us this time."

Facing up to a mob of angry-looking people is intimidating even for an experienced officer. It needed cool heads. Things could get ugly quickly.

A young couple were marched to a criminal transport bus. A slight, red-faced woman was pushing back while her partner told her to be calm.

It felt unreal. Like we were in some kind of theatrical production.

Captain Hank Frederson stood behind a line of officers. His gruff voice was amplified through a loud hailer.

"The owners want everyone off this site. That means you."

"The shipyard is making money. Coffi can't do this," a heavy set man in shorts and a red t-shirt shouted.

"We've got lawyers coming," another voice said.

"Okay. We tried it the easy way, now for Plan B." Hank said.

I saw Karl Rieper's face under a riot helmet. There was a volunteer Sheriff's star on his arm. He looked at me and pressed his tongue against the glass of his visor. He tapped his extendible baton against his leg like he was waiting for the fun to start.

We moved forward in a line towards the protestors. Most of them stayed put.

Two cops grabbed the heavy set man in the t-shirt and marched him towards the waiting, criminal transport buses.

A white-haired man with a Colonel Sanders beard stood with his arms crossed. Rieper swiped his baton against the man's head, knocking him to the ground.

Everyone started to shout and push. A young woman knocked into Rieper. He shattered her nose with the heel of his hand.

Most of the protestors had cops on them and were herded out of the shipyard into the waiting buses.

The man in the business suit stood on his own. Rieper downed him with a single punch and raised his foot to stomp his rib cage. I swiped the back of Rieper's leg. He fell backward.

"This isn't right," the businessman said, as I helped him up.

Someone barged into me, and I fell forwards. Rieper stood over me.

"You stupid bitch! This is way above your pay grade."

As I packed up my riot gear, dispatch gave the Venice code for 'animal problems' in the old folk's home down by Slaughter Lake.

Chapter Six
The Tatzelwurm

An expanse of still water reflected a dark, blue sky. Hemlock and fir trees fringed the lake's rocky shores. The Cape Misfortune asylum and a now-defunct Lutheran church had enjoyed these picturesque views since Victorian times. But the buildings here were now all run down except the nearly finished, glass-fronted Coffi Health Spa, bringing world class pampering to Venice County.

The Schöne retirement home served a dwindling client list. The once famous gardens were overgrown. The road had been pulled up when no one paid to repair the potholes. The imposing Victorian house and its outbuildings, once a genteel place to see out your declining years, had seen better days.

I stood at the front door and pressed the intercom.

"Yes?" a quavering female voice inquired.

"Sheriff's Office. You called 911."

"Follow the path. Herr Büchner is down there."

I walked through the garden to an open-fronted barn where an old man sat on a wooden dining chair.

"Herr Büchner?"

The man waved his hand towards a row of animal pens.

Two gutted pigs lay below a sign that said, "Feel free to pet the animals." A few strings of intestine hung loosely from empty rib cages. Wide, bite marks punctured scraps of loose skin. In the next pen, blood-stained fleeces lay in the straw.

"Any idea what could have done this, sir?" I asked.

"A tatzelwurm," the old man said.

A tatzelwurm was a mythical creature – the top half of a cat with the body of a snake.

"Unfortunately, I can't put imaginary creatures in my report."

I remembered Grandma Dollar telling us the settlers, who sailed to Cape Misfortune, came to make a utopia, but they brought themselves with themselves. The myths were just transported from one set of woods to another.

"It came in with the Weasel this morning," Herr Büchner said.

"I didn't know we had one."

Even reasonable people around here get jittery when the weasel fog comes, like people who don't believe in ghosts anymore still jump if they hear a noise on a dark night.

"It was very thick. It came for a few minutes during the night."

"What about a wolf?" I said.

"It would have to be a pack of them to eat all that. Unless it was the Stinkwolf."

"Also mythical."

The old man looked at me coldly.

"Are you Cape?"

"Born and bred."

"You should know better. You know about animals?"

"I grew up on a farm."

"You ever seen anything like this?"

"No."

"I have. In the early 70s. That was a tatzelwurm. People saw it."

I sighed.

"I'm going to get you in touch with Andi Malone, the Park Warden. See if she can help."

"Another woman."

"Another trained professional, Mr. Büchner."

The old man looked around the barn.

"You know the toddlers from the school up the way come here."

He put his head in his hands and wept. When I got in the patrol car, I realized I was a couple of miles from Bliss Schneider's apartment.

Despite my advice to Elliott, I paid a visit.

The street was a row of unremarkable 1960s brick buildings, the sidewalks outside lined with trees. A few people sat on chairs outside their doors, enjoying unexpected afternoon sunshine.

I parked down a side street and put a dark hoodie over my uniform. I ambled up the sidewalk to a tree opposite Bliss's house.

A van was parked outside the door. Bliss issued orders to a removal man in between talking on her phone. Her normally luscious mane of blonde hair was hidden under a baseball cap.

She looked over in my direction.

I felt a hand on my shoulder.

"Why are you hiding your uniform?" Boone asked.

"What do you care? Why are you sneaking up on me?"

"What do you think Sergeant Ambrose would say about wearing civilian clothes and illegally surveilling recent crime victims?"

"I'm having lunch."

"Where is it, then?"

"What?"

"Your lunch."

"I've eaten it. What are you doing here?"

"How did your back window get busted?"

"Piece of gravel."

"Where?"

"Up by Slaughter Lake," I lied.

"Cass, not everyone is cut out to be a police officer."

The injustice of that tingled all around my body.

Then Bliss stood in front of us, smiling broadly.

"Shouldn't you two be out directing traffic somewhere?"

Neither of us spoke.

"Cassie, didn't know you were back on the force. Thought they would have let you go, you being in the asylum or whatever it's called nowadays. What brings you to my neck of the woods?"

"We were just leaving," Boone said.

"You moving house, Miss Schneider?" I asked.

"I'm moving to a property by Wish Bay."

Boone tugged the back of my hood.

"We'll be on our way."

"Well, you two lovebirds take good care," Bliss said. "Because the Cape can be a dangerous place."

"Did that sound like a threat to you?" I asked, when we got to my car.

"No. She was talking about her own experience. Stay away from her, Cass. Whatever you are doing, stop it."

I woke up early the next morning. I didn't want to get lost again. I needed this job. I wanted my farm back. I had always wanted it. And a normal life, whatever that was. All of it.

Chapter Seven
Whistler

At mid-day, I dropped the Interceptor off at the Police Repair Garage in Venice City. The mechanic, a pony-tailed ex-cop called Jennings, raised an eyebrow at my story but took it no further.

"Come back in an hour," he said.

Venice City was on the mainland, so Cape folk considered it a different country. It was the ugly twin of Bandon, a town on the other side of the Shell River. Bandon took the lion's share of the fishing, hiking and beach crowd. Venice City, despite the determined efforts of the local council and law enforcement, attracted mostly trouble.

I zipped up my duty jacket. A long line of buildings looked out on the coast. Low clouds hung in the sky, threatening rain.

I ambled along a wooden boardwalk that ran beside the rocky waterfront. This had been a famous, oceanfront walk. In better times, it hosted a cranberry festival where my family had sold our berries. Now the coffee shops, and department stores, were closed. A few determined survivors still sold knick-knacks.

The ocean looked beautiful as ever, though. Surf roared around far-off, sea stacks. I had got lost in the bars of this beach resort before I met Boone.

Even then Venice was fast becoming a ghost town. It was going missing, like all the abductees. Alleged abductees.

I passed a garishly-painted, seafront bar I used to drink in. A regular recognized me and raised his glass. I waved back.

The rain came down hard. I jogged towards the striped awning above the door of the Venice City Arts center. It was a small, square building, whose brickwork was painted black. The door was open. A poster rested on an easel in the foyer. A man floated on his back above an exploding building. Lettering underneath said, 'The Levitator – all this week.'

"You want to come in out of the rain, Deputy?" a voice said. "The one o'clock show starts soon. Frankly, we need the numbers."

A man stood in the doorway, his tall, slim frame dressed in a black suit and turtleneck sweater. He had pale green eyes and a mop of dark hair.

"Thanks, but I'm on duty," I said. "You the Levitator?"

He bowed.

"Charlie Playfair."

His hand was cool and the handshake firm.

"You design the poster?" I asked.

He looked at my name badge.

"Have I met you before?"

"I don't think so."

"Were you involved in the Valkyrie bank thing?"

"I was. Your poster reminds me of something. Can you really fly, Mr. Playfair?"

"Call me Charlie. Come on in, see for yourself. Come later when you're off duty."

He reached in his pocket and took out a ticket.

"Compliments of the house, good for any performance you want," he said.

That night, I couldn't sleep so I climbed into the Interceptor. The patrol car had become my bat-cave. It had everything you would ever want to know about anybody and an unlimited data allowance.

Surprisingly Charles Hamilton Playfair aka 'The Levitator' had been a detective in the nearby Douglas

County Sheriff's Office. He was a model officer with commendations for bravery. He was now registered as a missing persons investigator in Venice.

I checked the Internet for Wish Bay properties. Only two were for sale, both more than a million. It could be an inheritance, a lottery win, she might be renting but Bliss Schneider was moving up in the world.

I dozed off in the front seat. Crashing sounds in the cranberry bogs woke me.

Whoever was out there made loud, guttural grunts. It sounded like our pet hog, Whistler. He used to bellow when he was hungry, which was most of the time. He was a friendly animal. But he was long gone. He went missing a week after Dad disappeared. His body washed up on Wish Bay. Buzz Everett returned him to us in a cardboard box.

I got out of the car. The moon was bright and full. A cold wind came in from the Pacific. The tall weeds in the ruined bogs rustled. I found a trail where the foliage was pushed apart. It led to a choked up bog with a single hoof print on the mud floor.

Then I heard something. Another grunt. Do animals even have ghosts?

"Whistler?" I called out.

I looked at my house. There were ghosts there, but not of people. The Prize was haunted by my memories of the thousands of moments my family had shared. Maybe coming back here was a mistake.

And had the window to Aggie's room been open earlier?

I opened the back door and went inside the house for the first time in years. The kitchen and the big room beyond were bare. Just a few strips of carpet and floorboards.

A window clattered upstairs. I climbed creaking stairs to the door that still had 'AGATA'S ROOM' written on it in marker pen.

I pushed the door open. The room was empty. A piece of lace curtain fluttered in the breeze. The open window banged a couple of times.

As I closed it, something flew high over the cranberry bogs, silhouetted against the moon. It didn't look like a bird or a bat. I have to report, even though a reasonable person wouldn't believe me, it looked like a pig.

Chapter Eight
Cath

Creak-thud. Creak-thud. Kurt and Francesco Deakins started yanking wooden planks off the house early.

I looked out of the tent. The see-through, plastic sheets wrapping the house flapped in the breeze like the flags of a forgotten battlefield.

For the first time since being blown off the bank roof, I imagined a possible future no longer freighted with unbearable suffering. On the cinema screen of my mind's eye, I saw out-of-focus figures. New people in my life. Kind people, I hoped.

Most mornings I went into work a few minutes early to use the little shower in the Needlepoint bathroom.

Today Ann was already behind her desk. Someone else stood in front of it. The stranger turned and smiled at me. She was about five feet high. Her lips were luscious, her skin smooth and her cheeks rosy.

"We just looked for the SUV and couldn't find it. Dan Ridley tells me you've been taking it home with you," Ann said.

"My car broke down."

"Maybe you should get yourself a new one rather than using county property."

"Yes, ma'am. I'm sorry."

Ann stood up and filled a mug from the coffee maker on the filing cabinet.

"Mrs. Postulart heard a gunshot early Monday morning on the Wish Bay cliffs. Know anything about that?"

"No."

"Said she saw a Sheriff's car on the Lookout parking lot."

"Oh, wait. I did go up there, briefly."

"Why?"

I hesitated.

"I needed to check something on the mobile computer unit, so I parked there."

"Mrs. Postulart said your vehicle almost went over the edge of the cliff. The wheels were spinning so hard smoke came off."

"I overshot and had a little trouble getting back up the bank."

Ann stared at me, suspicion in her eyes.

"Did you discharge your weapon?"

I kept eye contact with her and tried to avoid the body language police officers are trained to detect when people are lying to them - blinking, coughing, and covering the mouth.

"No."

Ann took a pair of latex gloves from a box.

"Will you hand me your gun?"

I did so. The other cop, who still hadn't been introduced, turned away to look at the bay.

"Would you mind if I sent this to forensics, see if it's been discharged recently?"

"No, ma'am. The last time I drew, it was a convenience store robbery in Valkyrie last year. For which I got a commendation."

"A lot has happened since then."

I actually owned two Glock 21 automatics. I bought the first with my own money while the county dragged its heels upgrading to the newer model. The second, more modern gun I used, on the back window, was currently hidden beneath my tent. If Ann sent this one, they might check the serial number, and know I had another.

"How many bullets in the clip?"

"Thirteen, I think."

"You think."

Ann ejected bullets from the magazine.

"The repair shop in Venice City said you took the Interceptor in."

"That's right."

"For a broken back window."

"Correct."

"How did it get broken?"

"A piece of dirt on the road."

Ann finished ejecting bullets and handed them back to me with the gun.

"You are on very thin ice," she said.

Then she pointed at the new deputy.

"Meet Corporal Cath Claybourn. She'll be working out of Needlepoint and going on patrol with you."

Cath held out her hand.

"Pleased to meet you. I'm interested to find out if all the wacky stories about Cape Misfortune are true."

"Folklore is a serious waste of police time here," Ann said.

Corporal Claybourn clapped me on the back.

"Right, shall we saddle up, partner?"

We headed out into the salt marshes. The sky was a gunmetal gray.

"Hear you were caught up in that bank thingumajig," Cath said.

"I'd prefer not to talk about it, ma'am."

"Understood. You can call me Cath. You a married lady?"

"No. But you already know that if you worked in Venice City."

"Sure, I know Boone."

"I don't want to talk about that either."

"Just so we're straight, I had no idea what Ann was going to say to you. I was very uncomfortable in there."

"So was I."

Cath laughed. Her eyes opened up wide. She made alternating braying, giggling noises.

She's going to take getting used to, I thought.

At the end of the shift, I found Boone in the office, stood in front of Ann's desk, arms behind his back.

"Okay, is it true you two illegally surveilled Bliss."

"No ma'am. I stopped to get a coffee in the area."

Ann looked at Boone.

"I saw Deputy Dollar's patrol car. It was lunchtime, and we had a chat. I had no idea Miss Schneider lived nearby."

"A cozy lunchtime chat, with your recently divorced wife who just happened to be hanging around outside Miss Schneider's old residence. I am disappointed in you, Deputy Washienko."

Boone gazed at the area over Ann's shoulder.

"If anything like this happens again both your careers in law enforcement are over."

Boone gave me a lift to the farm. He gave the impression he wanted to talk about something but he didn't.

Chapter Nine
The Levitator

This is the twenty-first century, right? When a showbiz guy, at a magic show, correctly guesses your card we know he has misdirected your attention from what actually happened. But I saw real magic on the rooftop. I hoped to experience it again.

Parents and children were crammed in the small arts center auditorium, sitting in tiered seats around a bare black stage. I found a place at the back.

The lights dimmed. A spotlight came up on Charlie Playfair. His dark hair was scraped back making his face look chiseled. A tailored suit and black, silk shirt covered his elegant frame.

"The essential elements of flying are a love of landscape, a contempt for the laws of physics and a feeling of separateness," he said. "Tonight, I will show you how, if you believe anything hard enough, you might achieve the impossible."

Charlie took out a wad of yellow Post-it notes and made some swift cuts with a pair of scissors. He held out his palm. The papers had become beautifully-shaped butterflies. The wings on the top note curled and trembled, as if in a breeze. Then hundreds of paper creatures flew into the audience. One circled around me before falling into my lap.

More magic followed. A card trick. Then Charlie locked an embarrassed mom into a trunk and stuck swords into her. Two children came up on stage, walked into a closet and disappeared.

I started to wonder if there would be any levitation.

Charlie brought a basket onto the stage. He pulled out a coiled length of rope, held one end and threw the other into the air, where it stayed upright, suspended. He climbed up, waving from the top.

The lights went off. When they came up, Charlie lay on the floor. A gentle breeze rustled the audience's program notes. The Levitator's body rocked from side to side. Slowly at first. Then faster until it became like a speeded-up film.

Charlie rose off the ground. There was a gasp from the audience. The ex-detective rose six feet up and bobbed for a while. His dark shirt rippled as if he was submerged in water. Then, impossibly, he floated over the delighted audience as if dragged by an unseen current – so like what I remembered the figure on the roof.

I stood up. I could see no wires. Charlie drifted past the overhead lighting rig. He stopped beneath an open skylight in the ceiling. Then, as if on the swell of an ocean, a mysterious tide carried him out of the window.

The children screamed with delight. I felt a tap on my shoulder. The Levitator sat in the seat behind me.

"Thanks for changing your mind."

He was totally relaxed, as if we were drinking tea on a lawn somewhere.

"Pretty slick," I said.

"Can I buy you a coffee?"

He brought take-out from the theatre foyer. We walked along the promenade. The sky was a dirty grey. A hole in the clouds opened. Orange rays from a low sun shone through like a flashlight, illuminating a patch of the ocean far from the shore.

A gull swooped through the air in front of us, hoping for something to eat.

"Sorry, fella," Charlie said.

"Were you on the Kommerz bank roof when it exploded?"

He watched the gull swoop over the rocks.

"I was a couple of years above you at Valkyrie High," he said.

"I don't remember you."

"Charlie Playfair isn't my real name. I was called Andrew Hadman."

I thought for a moment and got a flash of a Goth teenager in a long, leather coat who always walked with his head down.

"I remember you," I said.

"When I left school, I settled in Douglas County, thought I had escaped the Cape forever."

"What brought you back?"

"Someone I love worked here. My boyfriend. He went missing."

"Sorry to hear that. During a fog?"

"Of course."

"My grandma said sometimes people use the fog to go away."

"Not Patrick."

I looked out at the water.

"Were you on the roof, Charlie?"

He thought.

"First, a story. A Cape Misfortune woman tells a man sitting beside her on a plane they are about to crash. She is clairvoyant, a descendant of Cape witches. She had a dream. The man was from the Cape and believed her. He asked, 'How do we stop it?' She said, 'Hijack the plane.'"

Charlie looked at me.

"Well, did they?" I asked.

"The man and woman were my parents. The plane crashed. Killed most of the passengers. By some miracle, they survived."

"I have a feeling you're not going to tell me if you can fly," I said, emptying my coffee into the sea.

He caught my wrist.

"Cassandra, I can see a plane crashing. I'm on it. You're on it. You and the other guy on the roof, Elliott Hands. And your ex-husband."

His green eyes looked stricken.

"I need to know whose side you are on, Cassie."

"You were good in there, Charlie. Stick to levitation."

I walked down the promenade.

"There's something terribly wrong in Cape Misfortune," Charlie said.

"Tell me about it."

"Someone has been rewriting history here in a big way."

Later, I crawled into my sleeping bag and munched on a slice of cold pizza. Rain pattered on the tent. It didn't lull me to sleep. I kept thinking of Charlie's warning. I tossed and turned until dawn broke and Francesco Deakins gave me a lift to work.

Chapter Ten
Narwak

At eight o'clock, Cath Claybourne drove the SUV over the northern Valkyrie hills. It was warm, unusually so for early April. The soil was thin here and the grass would turn honey-colored in the summer.

We parked by a quiet ocean and walked along a stone pier to a beige, police patrol boat. It had the Valkyrie wolf emblem on its aluminum hull.

Andi Malone came out of the canvas wheel house. She had watchful blue eyes that dominated a tanned, weather-beaten face.

"Morning, ladies," she said.

"Morning," said Cath, with the involuntary chortle she sometimes gave when meeting people.

We climbed in.

"Andi Malone meet Corporal Cath Claybourn," I said.

Andi handed us our life jackets and fired the engine up. The patrol boat sailed out into a gently, massing, turquoise sea.

"How far to the lighthouse?" Cath asked.

"About a mile and a half," Andi said.

Cath leaned over the side and stuck her hand in the moving water. It seemed to give her intense pleasure.

A gnarled mass of dark basalt appeared on the horizon. Long ago, a man called Ballantyne had used explosives to decapitate the sea stack's peak, leaving a plateau high above water level. The lighthouse tower on top now looked out over miles of ocean.

We moored on a stone jetty, built, I had read somewhere, by the Army Corps of Engineers. Gulls circled above us.

Andi led us up a flight of winding steps carved around the outside of Narwak rock. We had to stop a few times to pull driftwood blocking our way.

"Recent storm," Andi said.

As we neared the top, the world seemed precarious and dwarfed by massive forces. The Cape was a far-off line, hazy, and almost unreal.

I got a paranoid feeling someone was watching us.

"Anywhere else a boat could dock here?"

"No," Andi said.

"Who called this in?" Cath asked.

"Anonymous 911."

"Out here?"

Andi shrugged.

Out to sea, a long semi-circle of dirty cloud was moving our way. We crossed the decapitated plateau, smooth and flat almost like black ice, to an old building standing at the foot of the tall lighthouse tower. Wildflowers grew at the bottom of the walls.

Maybe someone was getting a kick from seeing the cops turn up, I thought. Watching from the mainland through a telescope. Or perhaps they came out here in a dinghy. Hiding in the rocks somewhere.

Cath looked up at the tower.

"Does this big old thing still work?"

Andi laughed.

"Decommissioned in 1956. It's a heritage site. The authorities are trying to sell it."

She pointed to the metal and glass lantern room at the top of the tower.

"This light could be seen for twenty miles or more, even with whale oil or kerosene."

She took some keys out of her pocket.

"It's not in the literature, but they built it for the weasel fog. The lighthouse keeper tooted on a steam-powered horn to warn the boats."

Andi didn't need her keys. The front door had been kicked down.

We went in. The room was cold and gloomy. A big desk was upturned. There were black, scorch marks in the corner where someone had lit a fire. Some half-burned brochures lay strewn over a wooden floor. All four of the old, leaded windows bulged outwards as if someone had beaten them repeatedly.

There were lines of spray-painted, black symbols over the walls – pictures of half-recognizable things – wolves, tatzelwurms, winged fae. The artist had thrown lumps of brown excrement around the room as a finishing touch.

I couldn't imagine any of the Cape criminals I dealt with regularly doing something so stupid. I thought whoever did this is not from around here. Boy, was I wrong on that one.

I climbed spiral, cast-iron stairs to the lantern room. The wind was blowing hard up here. Most of the old room's long storm-pane windows had been kicked out. I felt dizzy. Through those cracked windows and empty gaps, the ocean seemed to stretch endlessly.

Broken glass littered the circular, iron floor. Somebody had stamped on the magnifying lenses around the lighthouse lamp. Something glinted amongst the fragments. A knife, with a familiar inscription on the side. Berühre und versklave: touch and be enslaved.

"Hey. What you got there?" Cath asked, from behind me. "Wooh. Looks sharp. Could you bag it for me, sweetie?"

I stepped back.

"Help yourself."

She patted a pouch on her belt.

"I've used all my forensic gloves."

I knew what the blade was. I strongly suspected Cath did too.

"It's called a geschank," I said.

She giggled.

"A ge-what?"

"Cape German. Touch the knife, you become the slave of whoever forged it. I'm a little superstitious. You're from the mainland so you'd probably be okay."

I took out a pair of my own latex gloves and offered them to her. Cath didn't take them. This, I realized, was a dance we were having.

"The blade will always find a way to cut you, no matter how you hold it," I heard my grandma's voice say.

"Not sure who could trust a police officer who won't collect evidence from a crime scene," Cath said.

The first rain from an overcast sky gusted through the broken windows, dusting us with drops of water.

I heard Andi on the metal steps. I didn't want her to pick it up. I put my gloves on. But I imagined the blade nicking my flesh and darkness flooding my body. I took the gloves off.

"I'll tell Ann. Bag the evidence. That's an order," Cath said.

I shook my head.

"Go ahead and snitch. I'll tell her you didn't want to pick it up, either."

Another wave of cold rain gusted hard through the smashed windows. It was part sea-water and made my eyes sting. The blade sparkled amongst the glass. Cath's hand dropped on the grip of her pistol.

"Who will she believe? A known coward or a real mainland cop?"

Andi walked up the stairs.

"Okay, ladies, it wasn't in the forecast, but the weather has turned nasty. We need to be on our way."

Cath picked up the little knife and dropped it into an evidence bag.

"What a mess," Andi said, looking at the broken lenses. "You know, a historic log cabin in the state park got torched a couple of days ago."

"What's that got to do with this?" Cath said.

"It was on the shore where Narwak University is hoping to build the marine sanctuary. Coffi wants a major shipping lane there to service the new pipe."

Cathy snorted.

"How would burning down a log cabin help?"

"Makes Cape Misfortune less valued. Easier to develop."

Cath blew a raspberry.

"Hogwash and eye-white. Someone in your job shouldn't say things like that."

"Maybe," Andi said.

A booming smack came from the rocks.

"That's the first Narwak wave," Andi said. "Let's get moving."

Foaming breakers boiled around the jetty as we jumped in.

"I really don't know much about you, Cath," Andi said, while they were in the wheelhouse.

Cath scratched her nose.

"Grew up in Douglas County. Moved to Venice. Got married a while back."

'What does your husband do?" Andi asked.

"He works for Coffi."

"Doing what?"

"Engineer."

"You really never heard of a geschank before, Cath?"

Her lips pursed into the hint of a sly smile.

"I'm not from the Cape."

Later we drove through torrential rain to the Needlepoint office. Ann was eating a cheese toastie while watching TV. Bliss Schneider was on the news, talking modestly about her behavior during the bank robbery.

"She's on the payroll now. We love local heroes," Wesley Simon, the boyish Coffi Corporation President said.

"Good for her."

I met up with an old high school friend, called Laurie, after work. We ate out in Bandon. She brought her new baby with her. My thoughts strayed to Boone and our lost child, now an absence. I felt a jolt of agony when I recollected how completely he betrayed me.

I drank a beer on the back porch. It started raining.

I got into the tent, zipped myself into my sleeping bag and closed my eyes. The insistent tap-tap of rain on canvas grew heavy and repetitive, like the drums of Cape Misfortune's legendary, lost marching band missing since the war of 1812.

A ghostly hand unzipped the front flap of my tent. The smell of something rank wafted in. A bare-chested Ed Henderson crawled out of the storm.

"I do so enjoy my time above the stairs, even in bad weather. I must confess death can be a little tiresome."

His tattoos glowed orange, but there was a muscular body underneath now, dripping with rainwater.

"What do you want?" I said.

"All those meds Dame Teddy has got you on should be chilling you out, letting you go with the flow."

"You came here to tell me that?"

He examined his fingernails.

"Corporal Cath is more important in the general scheme of things than you are. A big hitter. In the days ahead, you'll need to let her do her thing. That's the word from on high. Or is it down low?"

He winked.

"Okay, messenger boy, could you leave now? You're stinking the place out."

His luminous tattoos flared and filled the tent with a dull orange light. A gob of faintly glowing spit hit the tin star on my folded-up, uniform shirt.

"You know, Cath and your ex-hubby are getting on real well in Venice City. I've been spying on them late into the night. She's a real comfort to that boy."

"Good. They deserve each other."

"You best behave, darling. The higher-ups are starting to worry they took the wrong sister all those years ago."

As Ed opened the entrance flap, I glimpsed the faint glowing shade of Whistler the hog staring back at me.

I laid my head on the pillow. This time the patter of rain lulled me into an uneasy sleep.

Chapter Eleven
Shooter

I woke to the sound of someone banging nails into wood. The smell of resin wafted into the tent. New timber replacing the old, beetle-chewed planks. A good smell.

On the Cape, it's wet and windy most of the year, but we have our seasons. The days were getting a little warmer as spring approached. This morning, the sky was clear and the sea breeze mild. Lately, I had even started to get on with my partner, Cath. Things were calming down. But I've never strayed far from trouble.

A voice came onto the radio.

"Shots fired at Valkyrie High."

"Misfortune 2 en route," Cath said.

An image of Elliott flashed in my mind. He was a teacher there. I tore up Seven Mile, lights flashing. When I parked, Cath grabbed my arm.

"Now, we wait," she said

But I had no time for her games. I ran into the school's square entrance building. The corridor was deserted. Maybe they practiced active shooter drills here, I thought. If so, kids would be hiding under their desks now; the main school buildings would be in lockdown. The shooter would be prowling outside.

I ran around out into a grass quadrangle.

Cath caught up.

"Wait, I don't want you messing things up."

There was a gunshot from the sports fields beyond the big gym building, I thought.

I remembered what Ed's ghost had said. Let Cath do her thing.

I ran around the side of the gym towards the sports fields.

"Cassie, stop. That's an order!" Cath shouted.

Two people were sprawled in the goal mouth of a soccer field, locked in a struggle. A blonde-haired boy dressed in black, tactical gear lay on top of Elliott whose gym kit was covered in blood. Elliott's hands were around his attacker's wrist. The kid had a pistol in his hand.

"Police, drop your weapon!" I shouted.

Elliott looked over, but the kid didn't. I ran over and tried to pry the boy's gun out of his hand, but it was slippy with blood and his grip was tight.

There was a bullet wound in Elliott's upper chest. The index finger on his right hand was missing.

"Cassie, out of the way," Cath said, from behind me. "I need a clear shot."

I turned. Her gun was aimed at Elliot's head.

"Cath, don't shoot. The guy on the floor is the vic; help me get the kid's firearm."

The boy's gun fired into the turf beside Elliott's head.

"Out of the way," Cath ordered.

I got my knee into the kid's back. I pulled his arm up and twisted his wrist. In a few seconds, the gun-hand released. I slapped a handcuff on his wrist.

Elliott had a hand over his face. I looked back. Cath was aiming at him.

"He's the victim. Help me hook the kid," I said.

The shooter turned to me.

"You're really screwing things up, you stupid bitch."

He looked like butter wouldn't melt in his mouth. I grabbed his other wrist and slapped the handcuff on.

"You got the wrong guy," Cath said.

"You shoot him and I'll shoot you," I said.

Two Valkyrie cops ran around the side of the building.

"You threaten me?" Cath asked.

I thought I saw something bulge underneath the back of her jacket.

"No. I was talking to the kid."

Terry Cappin, a pot-bellied and usually humorous Valkyrie police sergeant, ran over.

I knelt beside Elliott.

"Better late than never," he said.

"You see any more shooters?"

He shook his head.

"Told you the bank wasn't an accident."

I spotted his severed finger in the grass.

"I knew I dropped that somewhere," he said.

Then he passed out.

The shooter, it transpired, was an eleventh grade student called Wilson Paderborn. He had model, law-abiding parents and no history of bad behavior.

Surprisingly, Boone made a point of coming over and asking me how I was.

Two hours after the incident, Hilary Fairhurst, the elected Sheriff of Venice County, strode through the scrum of police officers and EMTs with a television news crew trailing behind him. Hilly was all pink cheeks and a neatly trimmed beard. He put his hand on my shoulder.

"The people of our county are obliged to you, Deputy."

"Just doing my job, sir."

He turned to Boone.

"And the hero of the Valkyrie rooftop. Our County is lucky to have such fine young men and women."

Boone looked at his shoes.

"I didn't know who your boyfriend was," Cath said, that evening, on the journey back to Needlepoint.

I shrugged.

"I won't forget what you said to me, either."

"You going to make a complaint?"

Cath stared at me. Then she snorted and giggled.

"Let's say it was a silly old mix up."

It was Friday, so Dan Ridley was at the Needlepoint station getting ready for the night shift. He was a freckled, thick-necked gent who didn't talk unless he had to.

"A little birdie told me you threatened to shoot a fellow police officer," Ann said.

I looked over at Cath. She didn't look at me.

"This is Cape Misfortune ma'am," I said. "And, as you're always saying, you shouldn't believe everything you hear."

Ann shook her head.

"You are a walking disaster."

"You need a ride home, sweetie?" Cath asked.

"No, thanks," I said. "I'll finish up here."

Dan Ridley shook my hand and looked me in the eye for the first time since I was found alive on the Kommerz bank sidewalk. He didn't seem to share Ann's low opinion of me. A tiny light went on inside me somewhere. I pressed home my new advantage and asked for a lift to the farm.

Back home, I got into my sleeping bag and called the hospital. Elliot was stable, a ward nurse told me. They had helicoptered him to Coos, the biggest hospital on the coast, where they tried to re-attach his finger. He was still in a surgical recovery ward there, so no visitors or calls were permitted.

Chapter Twelve
Diedrich's Map

I climbed out of my tent. The ruined farm basked in pale sunshine. These fields and orchards would flourish again, I hoped. Familiar sounds of drilling and hammering came from the house.

I almost tripped on Charlie Playfair, asleep in the shadow of a Harley Lowrider motorbike.

I kicked his foot.

"You know this is private property, right?"

He opened an eye.

"Nice place."

"Glad it meets with your approval."

He stretched his arms and yawned.

"I am about to attempt cooking breakfast on my portable gas stove. Could I tempt you to something?" I asked.

"I never turn down food."

Charlie got up. We walked to the back porch where Francesco was laying planks over the newly-laid floor joists

We ate amongst the wildflowers by Charlie's bike.

"Who's paying for all this work?" Charlie said, pushing a fork of scrambled egg into his mouth.

"My mom," I said.

"And where is she?"

"Venice City."

"You see her much?"

"You ask a lot of questions."

Charlie smiled.

"I used to be a cop."

"And a pretty good one, I heard."

"One crime I couldn't solve. I fell in love with a Venice cop called Patrick Feuer. We got an apartment together. We were happy. Then, one day, he vanished."

"During a fog?"

"Of course."

"Don't tell me. He left his car on a Cape Misfortune cliff?"

"His bicycle."

"A cop going missing is quite a big deal, even here."

"There was an investigation, but no leads. Stories about Patrick started turning up in anonymous calls and emails to local journalists. They claimed he facilitated drugs coming to the coast from Portland. That he was on the payroll of a Venice City cartel, who killed him because he was greedy."

"Did you look into that?"

"I interviewed just about every criminal in Douglas and Venice. There was no cartel."

"Did you look up Patrick's old cases?"

"Yeah. The Venice detectives went through everyone but couldn't find anything. I gave up being a cop. But, a few months ago, I was going over my notes. One particular case had a vibe."

"A vibe?"

"Yeah, something that didn't feel right. A missing person case Pat worked on - a local farmer named Diedrich Leland."

"I knew Diedrich. He and his family used to sell cheese at the farmer's market when I was a kid."

"He complained someone was mutilating his dairy cattle. They came at night, stunned a cow and then cut out pieces of the body. Some nights it was the jaw, others the genitals or major organs. Whoever did it drained the blood and left symbols carved in the cow's skin."

"What sort of symbols?"

"Pictures of Cape folklore. The Stinkwulf, the Tatlzelwurm, the Hafferman, that kind of thing."

"I saw some of those on Narwak lighthouse yesterday."

"Really? Deidrich couldn't decipher them, neither could the cops. The farmer patrolled the place at night, but the killer always outwitted him. So, he set up surveillance cameras in his milking parlor and all over the farm. He spent his nights watching the video feed on his computer. A month later, someone in a black balaclava appeared out of nowhere and used a little knife to cut up a big cow. The mutilator looked like a woman, Diedrich thought. He claimed she drank the blood that puddled on the floor. Lapped it up like a cat. It was over in seconds, but she still found time to carve symbols into the animal's skin. Leland grabbed his shotgun and ran over but when he got to the shed, the mystery criminal was gone."

"Did she return?"

"A few days later. Diedrich missed her again, but followed her to a pickup truck and got the plates."

"So, who was the truck registered to?"

"The Coffi Corporation."

I whistled.

"Let me guess. They denied all knowledge."

"They said the vehicle was stolen from outside their Valkyrie office a few days earlier."

"Anyone at Coffi report the theft at the time?"

He shook his head.

"Later, they offered a witness who claimed he saw it being stolen."

"What happened to Diedrich?"

"He started causing trouble. Put stuff up on the Internet about Coffi, including video of the mutilations. A local reporter picked it up."

"And let me guess," I said. "Diedrich Leland vanished."

"Left a suicide note on his cell phone."

"Why would Coffi want to mutilate animals?"

"Patrick thought they wanted Diedrich's land. Apparently, Coffi offered to buy, but he refused. His estranged wife sold it after he went missing."

"What happened to the farm?"

"Coffi butchered the cattle, shut down the milking parlor and let the land go fallow."

"Patrick carried on working the case, but after he went missing his supervisor, Hank Frederson, closed it."

"Handsome Hank."

"Venice County's golden boy and almost certain, new Sheriff."

Charlie stood up.

"You want to go for a ride?"

"I don't have a helmet."

"I always carry a spare."

"Where to?"

"A magical mystery tour."

"I'm overdosing on mystery, Charlie."

He thought for a moment.

"Wish Bay."

We sped down country roads to the ocean's edge.

He parked on the cliff, and we walked down to the beach.

"When I re-investigated the mutilations, I tried to make sense of the symbols carved into the skin," Charlie said.

He took a phone out of his jeans pocket and showed me a photograph of a mutilated cowhide.

"I thought the markings were gibberish, but there is a system. Even now, I only understand some of it. Some symbols represent animals, some are concepts like danger or victory. A v-shape with a slash in the middle is a boat. It means to travel. I laid photos of the skins on top of each other and drew a line between all the instances of the travel symbol."

He swiped to the next photograph. It was a jagged horseshoe shape.

"Wish Bay," I said.

"Correct. Even down to Needlepoint rock."

I pointed to other shapes further out to sea.

"What are these?"

"Islands."

It looked like two large landmasses and a smaller one.

"I grew up here. There's nothing like that out there."

He scratched his chin.

"I grew up here, too, don't forget. I've heard the legends from old-timers. About the fog, the otherworld, the Isle of the Dead, all of that. This is a map."

"What use is a map to places that don't exist?"

He smiled.

"What about lunch? My treat."

We ate at a cafe in Valkyrie and Charlie bought a rocking chair from a junk shop.

"For the new porch," he said.

He strapped it to my back for the ride home.

We sat amongst the wildflowers. I liked talking to Charlie. He left late. That night there were no visits from angry dead people or phantom pigs, just ordinary darkness.

Chapter Thirteen
Agata

The next morning, I blew most of my wage packet on a 1983 brown and white, Dodge Ram pickup. I bought it from a silver-haired guy called Mike, who seemed to be an honest fellow. Then I drove up the coast to the Coos Bay Area Hospital and tracked Elliott down to a small room in the trauma unit.

I knocked on the door.

"Come in."

Elliott's cheeks looked hollow. His torso was heavily bandaged. Various diodes around his body were hooked up to a fleet of monitors.

There was a pink helium balloon tethered to the table beside his bed and a child's drawing on the wall.

"My nieces," he said.

"How's it going?"

"Bullet missed my heart by a few millimeters. This an official visit?"

"No."

"I'm honored."

I held up two cups of takeaway tea.

"Tea. Green or black?"

"Surprise me."

I handed him one.

"Any news on my shooter?" he asked.

"Local kid. Disturbed. Apparently."

"Was he by any chance under the care of Dame Teddy Champion?"

"Why do you ask?"

"Because the previous maniac who tried to kill me, Ed Henderson, was."

"Dame Teddy treats lots of local folks. But yeah, he was."

Elliott nodded.

"How's the hand?" I said.

He held up a heavily bandaged finger.

"The bullet took an inch or so off the finger. Won't be able to pitch for a while. Thanks for finding it."

"I'm glad you're alive."

"Me too. Cath pointed that gun at me an awfully long time."

"She did."

He picked up a copy of the Venice County Patriot and threw it over to me. The headline said, 'Bank hero starts a new job.'

"Any news on Bliss?"

"Moved to a mansion overlooking Wish Bay. Just started working in public relations for Coffi."

He took a sip of tea.

"You own a gun?" I said.

"Me? No. My dad shot himself. Put me off firearms."

"Sorry to hear that. But these are strange times."

I held up my spare Glock. He frowned.

"My trigger finger's out of action."

"Can you shoot left-handed?"

"You expecting trouble?"

"I honestly don't know."

He shook his head.

"No, thanks."

I drove home in a gathering twilight. The clouds were a bruised purple, looking beaten but defiant at the same time.

I jammed my foot on the brake. There was a girl on the rocky beach beside the road. I knew her.

Outside, cold spray clawed at my face. Below me, dark rocks were pock-marked with tide pools. Surf tumbled by the water's edge. The low sun reflected on the ocean in a red line, like a scar. Out to sea, thick fog engulfed Needle Rock.

My eyes adjusted to the twilight. I saw the young woman kneeling by a tide pool. Her pale fingers rippled the surface of the shallow water. Her look of hunched concentration was so familiar.

My sister. My sister when we searched for oysters and crabs.

"Aggie!" I shouted.

The figure turned her face toward me. It was so like my own. Unmistakeable. But her dark, violet eyes were lifeless. She opened her hand and showed me a spider crab.

I climbed down the rocks to the beach, slipping on a patch of loose scree and tumbling into a basin of water.

When I surfaced, Aggie stood at the edge of the pool, staring at me. Behind her, the purple and orange sky started to ripple and shine like a vast ocean. I held out my hand. She turned and ran.

"Please, Aggie, please." I followed her across the tidal flats faster than I ever ran in my life.

I had become so unsure of things, I doubted what I saw, even as it was happening. I wanted proof to release me from the doubt that had seeped into me. About my own sanity.

My sister ran towards the wall of surf thrown up by the sea hitting the rocky shore. She stopped for a second at the water's edge and looked back. Then her body was engulfed in foaming water.

A weasel fog closed over the shore.

I ran into the erupting surf and emerged in the ocean. I glimpsed my lost twin ahead of me, obscured in a haze of fog.

"Agata," I said. "Please."

A wave hit me so hard, I turned a circle under the water. When I surfaced, she was gone.

I looked for her until the cold water numbed my brain. When I got out the beach was so foggy, it took me a while to find a slope up to the road. I slipped a couple of times, sliding back down to the rocks.

I crawled into my truck and lay on the seat. An exhausted sleep overcame me. I dreamt I was a shorebird, high above Wish Bay. An army of dark figures marched out of the water.

When I woke it was night, and the fog had gone.

I stopped at Needlepoint station to check something on the patrol car's mobile computer that was bugging me.

Bliss Schneider's oceanfront mansion had belonged to a man called Santiago Haverford-Grainger. Perhaps unsurprisingly he had gone missing in a fog. His nephew and heir had sold it to the real-estate arm of the Coffi Corporation.

I should pay it an unofficial visit, I thought.

Chapter Fourteen
The Missing Wessendorf

It was nearing the end of a long shift. The air was close. Dark clouds lay over the Cape like algae in a stagnant pool.

"Report of a break-in at the Mausoleum on Wish Bay," a dispatcher's voice said.

Cath gave me a toothy grin.

"Gotta love Cape Misfortune."

She was her old, friendly self again.

I had lived my life on the Cape. This would be my first time inside the wall of dark stone that ringed the grounds of the old Wessendorf house.

It started to thunder.

"Wow," Cathy said. "Spooky! Love it. You don't believe in ghosties, do you?"

She tickled my armpit. I nearly drove into the marsh.

We stopped outside a pair of iron gates, which swung open. A tall figure in a plastic poncho beckoned us in and directed us to a weed-choked, parking space.

The mausoleum, at the bottom of the hill, once served as a family burial ground for the old house. It was now a condemned ruin at the top of the hill. The first Cape millionaire, Julius Wessendorf, built his stately pile on land overlooking Wish Bay vacated involuntarily from the Shell tribe.

The old Wessendorf house, from down here, looked like a wounded animal hiding behind the overgrown trees. A cliff collapse during a storm in the 80s left it a precarious few feet from the hungry sea. The once graceful architecture and broken columns gave it the air of a more ancient ruin.

The figure in the poncho hobbled towards us, using a wooden cane for support and puffing on a cheroot. He was an elderly gent, tall and solid-looking. His head was shaved, except for a square at the back from which a silver ponytail hung down to his shoulders. A pair of dark eyes studied us from behind oversized, green spectacles.

"Most welcome, ladies," he said.

He raised his stick and gestured for us to follow him towards an arched doorway in a granite wall.

"Are you Mr. Wolff, the janitor?" Cath asked.

"Depends who's asking."

We followed him down a flight of steps onto a broad, sunken avenue flanked on either side by elegant stone houses. Each had barred windows and padlocked doors.

"If you're thinking of moving here, don't. These cute little apartments are actually tombs," Mr. Wolff said. "A town of the dead. A part of the Victorian cult of death, apparently. Morbid if you ask me."

"How many people are buried here?" I said.

"Difficult to say. It was a big family. A lot of the bodies are missing. People say they go walkies during the fog."

Cath snorted.

"If that's true you should report it. Grave robbery is still a crime in this state," she said.

"No one has kept a tally here for a very long time, ma'am."

Mr. Wolff winked at her.

A dead yew tree lay across the sunken avenue. Our guide held up a branch to let us through.

"This place had a lot of fine looking cedar trees. All dead now, like everything else here, except weeds and rats."

He took us to an oak door, at the foot of a concrete dome, which looked at least eighty feet high.

"This is old Julius Wessendorf's catacomb."

He put his shoulder against a big oak door and shoved it open.

"Julius built it ridiculously big so his descendants would have to see it every day."

"What are we doing here?" Cath asked.

Mr. Wolff switched on a flashlight.

"I think old Julius' body is missing."

We followed him down a flight of stone steps.

Halfway down, he turned and graced us with a smile, under-lit by his flashlight.

"I wouldn't like to be here on a dark night."

I recognized that smile from somewhere.

We emerged into a round hall encircled by a grimy stone wall full of doors and barred windows. Dim light filtered through the dome's dirty central skylight onto a tiled, mosaic floor.

"The doors have seals on them, like in ancient Egyptian tombs," Wolff said. "String wrapped around wire. Strange thing. The seals are fine, but the coffins inside are usually broken into."

I peered through the window of one dark chamber. An empty lead coffin lay on its side.

"That was the third Mrs. Wessendorf's resting place," Wolff said.

He shone his light on an ornate structure stood beneath the dome's center. A heavy, coffin-shaped sarcophagus made of green marble sat on a massive square of black marble. Mr. Wolff shone his flashlight on the black slab. Carved pictures and runes were carved into the surface.

"This whole place is covered with symbols," Mr. Wolff said. "Julius was an occultist, you see."

One inscription was in Latin – 'J.W. NON-DISCESSISSE.'

"Julius Wessendorf. Not departed," Mr. Wolff explained... "Ironic, in the circumstances."

He shone his light on the floor. A marble lid lay in two pieces.

"You been up there to check if the body's gone?" I said.

"Me? No. I'm getting a little long in the tooth for that kind of caper. Besides, the Wessendorfs don't even pay me minimum wage."

"This is a waste of police time," Cath said. "These bodies have been missing for years."

"You have a ladder?" I asked.

"Just so happens, I do."

Wolff conjured a metal ladder out of the darkness.

He placed it against the marble block.

"Julius croaked in 1884. So, he probably won't be winning any beauty contests."

I climbed up to the sarcophagus and looked into the bowl. Even in the gloom I could see there was no body. It was just cob-webbed, moth-eaten velvet.

"Nothing," I said.

"No crime has been committed here," Cath said, as I got down.

"Grave robbery," Mr. Wolff said. "Is still a crime in this state, didn't you say, Corporal Claybourn?"

"How do you know my name?" she said.

"It's written on your badge."

Cath giggled, nervously.

"I used to be a Venice County cop," he said.

"Oh yeah. When was that?"

"A few years back."

"Haven't heard anyone mention the name, Wolff."

"No. My real name is Everett, Buzz Everett."

"Buzz?" I reiterated.

"Yeah. I let your family down once, Cassie. I won't do it again. Something you need to know about Cath, here.

She isn't human. Not, in itself, necessarily a bad thing. But she's a sociopathic killer. She'll kill you, eventually."

A gun fired. A hole appeared in Buzz's plastic poncho, below his left pectoral. A crimson stain blossomed over the t-shirt underneath.

I turned to see Cath, with a gun in her hand. Her eyes looked like nothing I had ever seen, like liquid silver.

I rolled behind the marble block. There was another shot, followed by silence.

I looked around the corner as Cath fell backward. Then she lay motionless, her skin turning a pale shade of blue. There was a bullet hole beneath her left ear. There was no blood. Instead, glowing liquid dribbled out and soaked her collar. Then her shirt burst open at the back. Corporal Cath Claybourn sat up, sprouting a pair of wings out of her shoulders - made of a thin, fleshy membrane.

She flapped them a couple of times and flew into the shadowy dome.

Buzz lay on the floor a few feet from me.

"Fae," he said. "Stupid of me. The Imperia is getting awful powerful if they can pass a fae off as human. Takes a lot of juice to pull that off. Masquerading as a cop. I've never heard of that before. A junk shop owner, maybe, or an eccentric tour guide."

Wings beat in the air above us. Twenty feet up, Cath closed one eye and aimed her gun. I rolled behind Julius's tomb. A bullet knocked a chunk from the corner of the marble. I leaned out and fired. Cath's head snapped back. A hole in the bottom of her chin leaked luminous dribble.

Her gun fell to the floor. Then she hit the ground between us. I found no pulse.

I ran upstairs to radio for an ambulance. When I got back, Buzz Everett was fighting hard for each breath.

"The world is changing. The Cape is just the start of a cancer that will spread."

"I wish you'd told me who you were, Buzz," I said.

"When I investigated your sister's disappearance, I ran up against powerful people here. Bad people. I got frightened. Turned tail, ran, and went east."

Cath twitched. There was a faint hissing noise as the fleshy wings retreated into her shoulders.

"The coroner is going to have a job explaining that," Buzz said, and laughed.

Then he screwed up his eyes in pain.

"Old Julius Wessendorf wanted immortality. And he heard of a place where the dead could walk again, for a price."

His eyes glazed over.

"Hang on, Buzz," I said. "Help is coming."

He came to for a second.

"You haven't touched any little knives recently?"

"No, of course not."

"Smart girl."

With that Buzz Everett's eyes rolled back and he was gone forever.

Chapter Fifteen
The Wagon

"Why shoot Deputy Claybourn, your partner? Why not Everett, if they were having a gunfight?"

"Because Cath shot first."

"It was dark down there. Are you certain?"

"I saw the bullet leave his chest."

"Because if you are lying, you could save everyone a lot of time by saying so now."

"The forensics will bear out my story."

"Cath's body went missing from the Venice City Morgue this morning, before a post-mortem. You know anything about that?"

"What? Don't be ridiculous."

"No one in Venice County law enforcement can figure out why Cath would want to shoot Buzz Everett. On the other hand, it is easy to see a motive for you shooting Cath. She had become a close friend of your husband."

"Ex-husband."

"Did you kill her out of jealousy?"

I looked out of the station window. The sky was aggressively overcast. Waves boiled around Needlepoint rock.

"No," I said. "Cath misrepresented parts of her life. There's no marriage or birth certificate or any record of her education."

"If that is the case, it will be looked into, but not by you. She was a popular officer. Plenty of people in Venice County liked her. I warned you. You are a menace to anyone you go out with."

"You finished?"

"No. You're suspended while the detective's office investigates the homicide of a serving police officer. And Captain Frederson wants another psychiatric evaluation. Now give me your gun, your badge and get out."

I went home and made toast on the gas stove then ate it sitting on the rocking chair on the new, back porch. The stars came out. They were beautiful, but more pitiless and remote than they had seemed in childhood. In the tent, I pulled the sleeping bag around me.

Rain tapped on the canvas like thousands of little fingers. The entrance flap opened. A stream of glowing urine arced in the air before hitting the groundsheet and evaporating in puffs of luminescent vapor. Ed Henderson stuck his head in and burped. He looked less human now. The pupils in his eyes were slitted, like a cat's. Or a snake's.

"You're still here, while the fragrant Cath Claybourn is gone. She was so much fun, unlike you. That's probably why Boone loved her so."

Ed put a finger against his nose and blew. A thin string of black goo shot out. A rank smell filled the tent.

"What part of letting Cath do her thing did you not get? You shot her down like the proverbial mangy dog."

"She killed a friend of mine. She was shooting at me."

Ed sat by the end of my bed.

"Old Uncle Buzz had it coming. He outwitted the powers-that-be for a spell but, believe me; no one gets away forever."

"He was a good guy."

Ed made gun with his finger and mimed shooting me.

"I should warn you. Cath's folk are awful warlike. Old Testament. Eye for an eye."

He tweaked my missing toe.

"You think a 'nobody' like you can go up against such important people? They'll crush you like a beetle under a stone."

The wind blew the tent flap open. Ed swaggered out.

I was woken early by crashing noises. Kurt and Francesco Deakins were dropping uncoupled, scaffolding poles to the ground.

"Just the plumbing and the electrics left to go," Kurt told me.

I ate a slice of toast and sat on my back porch looking for jobs in the local paper.

In the afternoon, I drove to Slaughter Lake for my psychiatric assessment. When I got out of the truck, rain drops stippled the water's surface, breaking the light into a thousand pieces.

"Hey, hey. It's the cop killer."

Karl Rieper stood behind me, wearing mirrored aviator glasses and a black muscle shirt that showed off his biceps. His gloved hands hovered above his twin holsters.

"You want to play a game of quick draw? I can guarantee you won't be as lucky as you were with my buddy, Cath."

"Why don't you Taser your pea-like brain, Karl? It might make you more intelligent."

He pulled out the Taser and pointed it at me.

"Why don't I try that out on you?"

As I walked past, he made a mock-lunge at me. I didn't flinch.

At the door, a wave of despair went through me. The creepy stone buildings, the gothic clock tower, all gave off a feeling of crushing antiquity and power.

I signed the visitors' book and walked along a gloomy corridor before knocking on a door marked, "Dame Professor Edwina Champion."

"Come right on in, beautiful."

The office was stiflingly warm. Dame Teddy sat in a leather armchair before a blazing log fire. Her hair was loose and hung over her tweed jacket. She gestured to the chair beside her. We watched the flames for a while.

"This is not the return of the prodigal daughter. Far, far from it. Handsome Hank wants your badge. And what he wants, he generally gets. Then, the great Cassandra Dollar will go back to being a drunk pouring drinks for other drunks."

"I shot in self-defense."

"Oh shush, you darling idiot, don't make me simply hate you any more than I already do. Cath was impulsive but a dear, dear patient and friend."

She sat back and sighed.

"I didn't know the wretched Buzz Everett," Dame Teddy said. "One of those tiresome, Cape conspiracy theorists."

She put a hand on my knee.

"A little birdy told me old Buzz was creeping about sticking his nose into other people's business. Did he pay you any secret visits and say why he was back?"

"No."

"Everett invented that silly story about Julius's body, so he could murder Cath."

"He said Cath was fae."

That made her eyes open. She sat back in her seat.

"Fairies in dreary old Cape Misfortune? How delightful."

The log fire spat out a few sparks.

"After Buzz shot her the first time, Cath flew up in the air," I said. "Like a bird."

Teddy hooked her thumbs and mimed a bird's wings with her fingers, imitating a bird cheeping.

"You tell anyone about that?"

"No."

"Wise owl. A trick of the light. False memory. Aunty Teddy make you all better."

Teddy kissed the tip of her index finger and pointed it at me.

"The stakes are too high, Cassandra. Any more stunts like this and I can't protect you."

"I came about my assessment?"

"A made up reason to see my favorite patient."

She smiled.

"Are you going to cause any more trouble?"

"Not if I can help it."

"Stand up, darling."

Dame Teddy put her arms around me and squeezed hard, her head between my breasts. Her hair smelt of beeswax. She pulled my face down and planted a kiss on my lips.

"Love a winner," she said. "I'll write a Post-it note saying 'sane as hell' to stick on your forehead. You can have your badge and pop gun back. Although, this time, try not to murder anyone."

When I got home, Elliott was on my porch steps, his arm in a sling.

"I saw a little blade in the weeds outside your front door," he said.

"You pick it up?"

He shook his head.

"Nope. I'm up with the quaint, European folklore here. Although I don't see why anyone would bother glamoring you."

"Why not?"

"You are already under their spell, aren't you? You do what you're told."

"I pick my battles," I said. "Like when I saved your life."

Elliott stood up.

"I'm going off the grid for a while."

"Where?" I said.

He hesitated.

"Some tribal land."

"You need me, just call."

He thought about that for a moment.

"Okay."

The following evening, I met Charlie for coffee in Valkyrie, and he talked about Patrick. On the way home, I took the coast road as the sun worked the last of its daily magic on the ocean's face. As the burning globe disappeared below the horizon, I saw a fog roll in over the water. Within a minute the coast was obscured.

I stopped and got out of my truck. A faint sea breeze ruffled the fog's hair and whistled quietly among the rocks as if through broken teeth, as if everything was empty and gone.

Horse hooves clopped on the road. The glowing outline of a wagon rode towards me.

An obese man sat in the driver's seat, flicking his whip at two horses. He wore a leather biker's vest a few sizes too small for him. The gang patches on it had symbols on them instead of words. Thick, horn-rimmed glasses magnified the man's humorous blue eyes. A sawed-off shotgun lay on his lap.

The wagon had bars on it, like a rib cage. A man sat inside, head cradled in his hands.

"You, in the cage. You okay?" I asked, as the vehicle got close.

The man looked up. It was Vincent Deary, his face caked in blood, his skin even paler in death. I ran in front of the wagon.

"Police. Stop your vehicle," I said, although I wasn't a cop anymore.

The horses whinnied. The wagon slowed. The big man wagged a nicotine-stained finger at me. Then he burped. A smell of rank flesh wafted over me. He raised his shotgun. I jumped out of the way, ending up sprawled on the rocks by the road.

The wagon picked up speed. Vincent cradled his head again. I ran after them, but it was too fast. The driver raised his hand and flipped me the bird.

I wanted to call 911, but what could I say - I just saw a dead ex-junkie on a ghostly, slave wagon?

Later, in my tent, when sleep didn't come, the ghost of Whistler snorted in the derelict bogs. I paid him no heed.

Chapter Sixteen
Devil's Hollow

The next day, Kurt Deakins handed me a letter from the mailbox he had just installed at the end of my drive. Venice County wanted me back.

Andi Malone called me early in my first shift.

Rain drummed on the tree canopy of the State Park. The tousle-haired park ranger shook my hand. Her face was grave.

"Good to see you back. Came across something. In Devil's Hollow."

Devil's Hollow. A canyon carved into the Cape Misfortune rock by a long-disappeared river. I had a flash of myself on a school outing, smoking my first cigarette and retching on some weeds while the boy I was with laughed at me.

We walked up the rocky path for a while. Thick groves of old-growth Myrtlewood, tall and multi-trunked, surrounded the hollow on both sides. Waist-high, giant ferns crowded on the former river bank.

"Wasn't this the lichtung where the fae held human slave fairs?" I asked.

Lichtung was Cape German for a forest clearing. Andi laughed.

"It's a dried-up canyon! Although an old-timer once told me the Hafferman followed the settlers to America and used to wait in the trees to kidnap unwary children."

"Is he the one who rode a six legged horse?"

"That's him. Big black hat; used a walking stick as a cudgel. You believe the folklore?"

"I'm really not sure what I believe."

Andi raised an eyebrow.

"Well, rest assured I'm the only witch in this forest."

She waded into a patch of ferns and pulled up a square of camouflage netting. The tops of three steel drums poked out of a muddy trench.

"I assumed they were narcotics," Andi said. "They sometimes use fifty-five-gallon drums like this."

We hauled one out. It made a sloshing sound. A triangular warning sign on the side said, US ARMY. HIGHLY HAZARDOUS CHEMICALS.

"Any idea what's in them?"

Andy pointed to an identification number on the lid.

"M-77. Mark 77. A modern variety of napalm. Illegal for civilians to own. Designed to torch enemy supplies, equipment, and structures. It burns very hot, and it's nearly impossible to put out."

"Any reason it would be here?"

Andi shook her head.

"We sometimes do a prescribed brush fire in October, but not with chemicals like this. There's enough in these babies to burn half the whole State Park."

"Who found it?"

"I did."

"Maybe I should call Homeland," I said.

"Looks that way."

Andi's right eye burst open. The sharp metal tip of a javelin kept going for a few inches, taking the ruptured eye globe with it. She looked surprised for a second, then crumpled. The long, wooden shaft sticking out of the back of her head had a faintly glowing inscription, 'To touch is to enslave.'

A shadow passed overhead, like a giant bird, and my skull exploded with pain.

I woke face down on bare rock. It was late afternoon judging from the sun. The back of my head throbbed. My first thought was I had been speared. But I was alive. I got up on my knees and retched.

I staggered around the hollow searching for Andi's clump of ferns. I found it but the park ranger's body was gone, along with the steel drums. The mud trench had been filled and carefully tamped down.

Poor Andi. Ann Ambrose was right. I was out of my depth.

I walked to the patrol car and drove until I got pick up for my phone.

"Cass?" Boone asked.

"I'm outside the state park. Someone hit me on the head."

"Go to the hospital."

"Andi Malone has been murdered. Can you meet me? I wouldn't phone you unless I was desperate."

Boone sighed.

"Andi Malone threw herself off the Narwak rock this morning. She texted her husband a suicide note. Washed up a couple of hours ago. Ham Rourke took the call. Said she hit the rocks. Real mess."

"I saw her die in Devil's Hollow. She was killed by a spear."

"My advice? Think for a moment before you call that in."

I stopped the car and sat on the Shell riverbank. My head ached. I need the Emergency Room, I thought.

Boone sat beside me. I thought of our happier times by the river.

"You okay?"

"I haven't been okay for a while, Boone."

"You've got blood on your uniform."

"Andi's blood. She was shot because of something she found in Devil's Hollow."

He sighed.

"Okay, I'll bite. What?"

"Barrels of military-grade, incendiary gel called Mark 77. She thought someone was planning to burn the park down."

"Who would want to burn the park?"

"The same people who broke Keyhole Rock and vandalized the lighthouse. The people who just killed Andi."

"Look, Andi killed Andi," said Boone. "I'll drive you to the ER."

They kept me in overnight. I dreamt I was flying high above a weasel fog. I could see everything through the mist. Each blade of marsh grass was a vibrant life rippling in the wind. The river flowed with enormous purpose. Stone figures stepped out from the sea stacks. The rock beds on the beach were full of algae and weed dancing to the same rhythm as the grass. The whole shore glowed. The water itself was alive – an ever-changing organism.

An orange light appeared over the headland. Fingers of fire caressed the Cape.

Chapter Seventeen
A Map of the Otherworld

When I got home from the hospital, I saw Charlie's motorbike on the back lawn. He was asleep on the rocking chair. I woke him up and told him about Andi.

"Should I come back another time?"

"No."

"There's something I'd like you to see."

We climbed onto his bike and sped over country roads to the cliffs above Wish Bay. The sky was pristine and cloudless. He parked and pointed to a speck on the horizon.

"You interested in finding out what happened to your sister?"

"Off the record? Of course."

"The old Wessendorf House is where it all started. We'll leave the bike. Don't want to broadcast our arrival."

We went along a cliff top trail between bushes and high grass, buffeted by strong winds. It reminded me of being a couple. I thought of Elliott's dark, kind eyes.

The front gate was padlocked. We walked in the shadow of the towering boundary wall, where overgrown scrub and bushes flourished.

"There was a security guard the last time I was here," I said.

"Buzz Everett."

"You knew Buzz?"

"Very well. I'm sorry he's dead."

"Me too."

"Security at this place is run by a firm in Valkyrie. The guy who patrols it is an ex-colleague. He's away today."

Charlie stepped into a tangle of vegetation. I followed. We squeezed between stubborn, prickly greenery ending up by a V-shaped collapse in the stone wall. Charlie climbed over.

"If we get caught in here, I'm out of a job," I said.

Charlie turned.

"Is that all you care about?"

"I'm here with you, aren't I?"

"Yes, sorry."

A line of untended, hawthorn trees cast a permanent gloom over this part of the grounds. Their gnarled branches looked like illustrations in a fairy story.

"You ever worry about going missing?" Charlie asked.

"Sometimes I feel I already am."

"You just took out the school shooter. You're a local hero."

"Most of my colleagues don't like me for shooting Cath. It was my sister who wanted to be a police officer, not me."

"What did you want to be?"

"A cranberry farmer."

He smiled.

"I always wanted to be a levitator. A guy whose feet never touched the ground."

We emerged into a sunlit meadow of tall weeds. Two lines of rusty metal ran through the middle.

"Railroad tracks," Charlie said. "Julius Wessendorf had a private extension built all the way from the Valkyrie docks."

The stone walls and turrets along the roof gave the old house a medieval feel. Even in morning sunlight, the silhouetted mansion looked like a castle under a severe curse. Moss and ivy had colonized most of the walls. Long rows of cracked, or empty, windows resembled broken teeth.

Steel-mesh security screens covered the doors and windows along the ground floor. Charlie stopped by a padlocked door cover and unzipped a small leather case. He wiggled two wires in a padlock, which clicked open.

"Not bad," I said.

"I learned from an old school copper by the name of Buzz Everett."

We went into the house.

There was a strong, musky smell of dead animal. We were in a dark corridor. Part of the ceiling had collapsed, leaving chunks of plaster on the black-and-white floor tiles. A rusty bicycle had fused with the metal radiator it leaned on.

We came out in a grand entrance hall lined with ornate, marble statues and gold brocade worthy of an abandoned French palace. Grey flagstones on the floor made it feel like a courtyard. The walls were paneled in wood. Each board had a different, hand-carved, floral motif painted in bright colors now faded with time. Two giant mirrors had lost their silver and were nearly dark.

A big, wooden staircase stood at one end of the room. The descending handrails ended in two carved statues of winged fae.

"Up we go," Charlie said.

The decayed tread boards creaked ominously with each step. I followed him to a square landing.

He pointed to a faded tapestry on the wall. The word 'Hiddensee' was written at the top.

"A Myrtlewood tree. It looks like the tree of life, but the branches slope down, so it's a tree of death. Now, look at the shape above the tree."

Charlie pointed to a familiar horseshoe-shaped line at the top.

"Wish Bay," I said.

"Correct. Now, look at the bottom."

Roots from the tree extended into the three islands on Diedrich's map.

"So, it's a map."

"The tree of death connects Wish Bay to the Otherworld. The small island at the bottom is the Isle of the Dead."

"That doesn't sound good."

"No. Best avoided. Go back up to Wish Bay at the top. See a little castle on the coast? A tower with turrets, like a chess piece?"

"Yes."

"That's here, the old Wessendorf house, where we are now. That tiny square in the castle represents a door."

He looked upwards towards a dark rectangle in the house's far-off ceiling.

"That's a door?"

"Follow me," he said.

Charlie jumped easily between safe areas on the rotten, stair treads. I tried to mimic what he did. After the third landing stair treads started to go missing. The jumps got steadily bigger.

"You sure this is safe, Charlie?" I said.

"None of this is safe."

The top landing had a dirty, cracked window that overlooked the untended grounds. The house was near the cliff edge on this side. A few feet of overgrown garden, then nothing.

Charlie was looking at the ceiling. The strange wooden door was twenty feet out from the landing in an expanse of cracked ceiling.

"How do we get up there?" I said.

He picked up a long window pole with a metal hook on the end. He swung it under the doorway until he caught a latch. A square door swung down from a single hinge. A knotted rope fell out. It dangled in the air ahead of us. Charlie hooked it and pulled it over.

I climbed up onto a rickety handrail and took the rope, making the beginner's mistake of looking down. It was a long drop to the courtyard.

"Do we really have to do this?"

"You'll be fine."

I placed my feet around a knot in the rope and swung out into the air, swinging back and forth until Charlie hooked the rope and steadied me.

I climbed slowly upwards, using the knots as footholds, until I reached the square opening and manhandled myself through. For a second, it felt as if I was in a bubble of light, made of sky. As my eyes adjusted, I saw I had climbed into a glass dome whose cracked, and grimy, panes were held in place by a corroded metal frame.

I stood up. Familiar-looking symbols covered a dark, wooden floor. A six foot long slab of undressed basalt stood in the middle of the room. A carving on the side said, 'To touch is to enslave.'

There were eight chairs set at equal distances around the room's edges. The seats were circles of polished black stone resting on rusted bronze legs. There were upright, metal hand grips at the end of each wooden armrest.

"The altar is a big geschank," said Charlie, as he climbed through the hatch.

"A geschank needs to be sharp."

"Look at the surface."

The top of the lintel had a sharp, bronze spike roughly corresponding to where the heart would be if someone lay on it. There was a circle of ancient, black gunk around it.

"Wouldn't want to take a nap on that," Charlie said.

"Ouch."

A brass easel stood at one end of the altar. It held a gilt-edged book. Charlie picked it up.

"*How to Speak with the Dead. A Practical Guide* by J.W," he said.

"Julius Wessendorf?"

"Privately printed," Charlie said, opening the book at the title page.

A sepia photograph showed a white-haired Wessendorf standing in the room we were in now, dressed in a dark robe embroidered with symbols. He stared at the camera with pale eyes. His left hand, palm open, offered the reader a silver geschank.

"What went on up here?" I asked.

"Buzz and I spent months trying to figure that out," he said. "Wessendorf called this place his Scrying Room. Scrying means viewing things at a distance, magically, like looking in a crystal ball or, in his case, a silver dish of Wish Bay tide-pool water and blood."

Charlie pointed to the symbols on the floor.

"A few of the symbols use Latin words. 'Fuga' or flight, combined with a circle means magical flying."

"Like levitation?"

"Yeah. Wessendorf spent years up here trying to fly somewhere."

A cloud swallowed the sun, making the domed room somber.

"Why?"

"Julius wanted immortality. He heard of a place where the dead could walk."

"Buzz told me that."

Charlie closed the book.

"I read about Buzz's disappearance and tracked him down to a shack in Dakota. Buzz had a lot of theories about the Cape. He knew about this room we're in now. Heard about it from an old-timer who worked here."

"So, what are we doing up here, Charlie?"

"You asked me if I could fly."

"I did."

"I have a confession to make. The flying in my show was fake. It paid the bills."

"It was good."

"Up here you can fly for real."

"What?"

"Buzz and I spent time up here using Wessendorf's book. Incantations and stuff. Nothing happened, we just felt foolish and mostly got the giggles. But, last February, I was very ill in Valkyrie hospital. I was delirious, and near comatose. There was a storm outside. The symbols I saw in here came into my head. They made patterns in my mind. Suddenly, my soul was plucked out of my body like a handkerchief from a top pocket. I was looking down at my body from the ceiling. I thought I was dead. But the cardiac monitor by my bed said I wasn't.

"Charlie."

"I tried to rejoin my body but couldn't. Suddenly, I was sucked through the window, which was closed by the way. Then I was floating outside the hospital. I saw there was a luminous cord between the heels of my spiritual and physical body, like an astral umbilical cord. I heard thunder out at sea. I tried to swim upwards but I just hung there in the fog. Suddenly, a strong tide dragged me hundreds of feet into the air. Then another current pulled me sideways. After a few experiments, I figured you had to find a tide and ride it to get where you wanted."

"I do that in the sea, sometimes," I said. "It's dangerous."

"I rode up high above the Cape. I went over Valkyrie town. I flew across the salt marshes, pulled by weird tides hundreds of feet in the air. Soon, I was over the water. I left the cliffs far behind and rode the spirit tides until I saw the shore of a frozen, snow-covered land. From Wessendorf's book, I knew it was the island called Winterland. Somehow, I knew a bitter wind kept the place in eternal winter. I sensed Patrick was there, in trouble. But

I was yanked back by my astral cord. Looking back, I think it was because the fog was lifting over the hospital. My soul was being reeled back."

"You said you were delirious. Could this have been a dream?"

He shook his head.

"No, because I did it again. From this room."

"What?"

"Buzz too. We saw incredible things. Now I want you to try it, Cassie."

"Don't you need a fog?"

"There's one on the way, I checked. And a storm."

Low clouds were eating up daylight in the sky above Wish Bay.

"On my last flight," Charlie said. "I went over Valkyrie riding the tides. But I saw something on a bank roof. Ed Henderson. He glowed. He was already partly spirit. Buzz said that happens a few minutes before you die. I saw the propane and explosives. I saw you and Elliott. You were both glowing too, partly spirit, about to die."

"It was you?"

He smiled.

"Yes."

Charlie pointed to one of the stone armchairs.

"Sit."

I did as he asked.

"These chairs are how Julius first contacted whatever is out there. Grab the metal grips at the end of the armrests."

"If Julius traveled in spirit, why is his body missing?"

"Good question. I don't know. Neither did Buzz. All the Wessendorf bodies are long gone. His wives, his children, even his pet dog."

The sky was like night. A flash of lightning lit a white fog climbing over the cliff edge.

Charlie sat down on the chair opposite and closed his eyes. A deep rumble of thunder rattled, dislodging a pane of glass that shattered on the stone floor.

I clutched the metal grips and felt an odd energy pass through them. It tickled at first. My arms felt faint. Then a torrent of cold, spiritual liquid burst through my body.

I watched the opaque spirit of Charlie Playfair rise through the glass dome.

I popped out of my own body, like a cork hurtling through the dome. I came to rest ten feet above the roof lying on my back. A powerful spirit tide dragged me over the cliffs. Beneath us, half-obscured by mist, great glowing waves rolled into the dark cliffs below the house.

The moon was out. It felt more significant, more important – a fierce presence through the clouds.

I saw Charlie ahead of me. He was on his front, using his arms for balance. I copied him.

The ocean roared around Needlepoint Rock. The surf, cresting on the edge of the waves, was so bright it was painful to look at. I couldn't get high enough and actually passed through the dark rock's tip.

Then we flew over the open sea, riding strange spiritual winds hundreds of feet over an angry Pacific. Our astral cords hung in the air behind us.

There were creatures below the water's surface. Not the whales you usually find on this stretch of coast. Two fantastically, long sea serpents slid through the deep water. One looked up at us with giant, inquisitive eyes.

Further out, glowing icebergs bobbed brightly in the wave torn water. A giant octopus tried to keep up with us using the suckers on its tentacles to pull itself over the seabed.

A line of radiant shore appeared on the horizon. It slowly grew into a vista of dazzling cliffs.

I saw a bright dot separate itself from the shore and fly towards us. The beating wings and golden hair belonged to someone I had hoped was gone forever.

Charlie slowed to a stop and we hovered high over the ocean. Cath Claybourn flew towards us, still wearing her torn Venice County uniform. She clutched the geschank I had refused to pick up at Narwak lighthouse, wrapped in its plastic evidence bag.

She was making for Charlie. He tried to fly around her towards the shore. I felt a wave of panic and caught a spirit tide that took me towards them.

Cath locked onto Charlie, grabbing his legs.

I knew instinctively what she wanted.

"No!" I cried out.

She had an arm around his legs. A geschank glittered in her free hand. She placed it against Charlie's ankle cord and sawed. He bucked frantically up and down.

I put my arm around her neck and tried to dislodge her. In that second, I made a curious discovery - we were spirit, and she was solid. But we could interact.

"Yippee!" Cath shouted, as the cord broke.

Charlie held out his hand to me. But his body was dissolving, out of control. An island appeared behind him. It had a single, dead tree beneath a mountain. He was carried on a riptide, tumbling into oblivion.

I felt Cath's arm close around my waist.

"You're next, Deputy," she said.

When the blade touched my cord, it hurt like a real knife on my flesh. I turned and kneed her in the face. She tumbled downwards, clutching her nose.

I looked for Charlie. He was gone, along with the island, so I turned and flew back across the ocean.

"Where d'you think you're going, sweetie?" I heard Cath say.

She was yards behind me.

I tried not to panic. I knew the tides of my ocean. If I could ride them down there, maybe I could do it up here. I found one and surged forward.

The familiar outlines of Wish Bay's cliffs appeared on the horizon.

The storm was worse by the shore. Swelling masses of tortured water smashed against the rocks. Sections of the cliff collapsed into the ocean.

A big chunk fell into the water beneath the old Wessendorf house, taking the corner tower of the west wing with it. Half the house was hanging over the edge of the cliff.

I flew through the dome into my seated body.

Charlie was on the floor, unconscious.

Cath Claybourn landed on the dome. The soles of her dirty, blue feet squashed against the glass. She knelt and ripped up strips of iron frame. Glass crashed onto the floor.

I looked at the open hatch in the floor. There was no way I could get Charlie down there.

Cath landed on my shoulders, knocking me over.

The whole building lurched to one side, rolling us both across the floor.

The room sloped at an impossibly steep angle. I could see the ocean, the rocks beneath.

As we slid, Cath crawled over me and put her hand around my neck. She lifted the geschank, ready to strike. I grabbed her wrist, got my feet against her stomach and kicked her through the hole she had just made in the dome, which was now on its side.

Then there was noise, water, and darkness. I grabbed hold of Charlie as the old Wessendorf house plunged into Wish Bay.

Light filtered through the smashed up dome.

Our bodies floated up to the surface of the waves.

I battled through the surf, pulling Charlie by his neck, choking on water.

A massive wave carried us high into the air, tossing us onto the rocky beach.

I dragged Charlie onto the cliff steps, beyond the reach of the seething, angry water.

Then I went unconscious.

Chapter Eighteen
The Mud Hen

A hand shook my shoulder. Dan Ridley stared down at me, his face etched with disbelief and concern.

Hands hoisted me onto a stretcher. An ambulance took us to Valkyrie.

Later, a junior doctor came out of the intensive care unit to say Charlie only had cuts and bruises.

"But we can't find any trauma to explain why he's nonresponsive."

I didn't tell her someone had just cut Charlie's soul from his body.

I got a taxi home. The ocean by Valkyrie was quiet now, like an animal sleeping it off after a kill.

The Prize's cedar wood roof shingles, hand-nailed by the Deakins, had survived their first storm.

There was a patrol car in the drive. Dan Ridley sat on the steps of my back porch, beside a hissing gas lamp. He had taken off his hat revealing neatly-cropped, red hair.

"You okay, Dan?"

"Why were you and Charlie out in the storm? I need a plausible story for my report. Ann wants you out."

He held up a witness statement form on a clipboard.

I shrugged.

"Okay, maybe it can wait until the morning."

He stood up.

"Wait," I said.

I left out the astral traveling. I imagined that, alone, would earn me an extended stay in a psych unit, and told him Charlie was following a lead on Patrick's case. We were in the attic room of the old Wessendorf house when it fell into the ocean.

Dan crumpled the piece of paper he was writing on and started a fresh one.

"You weren't in the old house. You went to Needlepoint station to volunteer in the storm. You saw Playfair's motorbike on the cliff top and went down to investigate. You found him unconscious on the steps. The wind blew so strong you fell over and hit your head."

"How d'you know about Charlie's bike?"

"I saw it. That's why I went down the steps and found you."

Dan held out the statement for me to sign.

"This isn't much better than my story."

"Might save your job, Cassie."

I signed the statement.

"I think this is the longest conversation we've ever had."

"Nothing personal," said Dan. "My mom used to say I was quiet because I fell out of an apple tree when I was eleven."

He lit a cigarette. The flame cast a flickering light amongst the dark shadows of the ruined, cranberry bog.

"I didn't know you smoked."

"I don't. Not when I'm in uniform."

Dan looked out into the darkness.

"Have you noticed we have a vandalism problem on the Cape?" he said.

"I've attended a few call-outs."

"You ever arrest anyone?"

I shook my head.

"Last week, I saw a young man spray painting symbols on the Valkyrie war memorial. I chased him into someone's garden, took him to Valkyrie police station and booked him. Next day he skipped bail. I say to the Valkyrie cops, who bailed him? They give me the name of a bondsman in Venice. I pay a visit. The bondsman has disappeared. They both had a fake identity, complete with bogus social security. It takes money to pull off stuff like that."

Dan looked genuinely angry.

"My grandpa's name is on that memorial. Why is it always monuments and protected places? A tunnel in the old gold mine collapses for no reason. An abandoned oil tanker with zero documentation spills its load over the Venice sand dunes."

"You think there's a pattern?"

"You ever work with Andy Rheinoldz, the Valkyrie cop Ed Henderson murdered?"

"A couple of times."

"Very down-to-earth feller. If he said something, you took notice. He thought powerful people were deliberately running the Cape down."

"Why are you telling me all this?" I said.

"Because, and don't be offended by this, I'm not sure you have a future in law enforcement here. You don't do as you are told."

"So why tell me, then?"

Dan stood up and pinched his cigarette's glowing end between finger and thumb.

"Because fixing things around here will need a few people who don't do what they're told. Good night, Deputy."

With that Dan went off into the night.

Later, I dreamt Charlie was falling through the darkness with nothing to hold or hang on to.

I got a text from Elliott, in the morning, to bring a wetsuit and meet him on Ukobach beach in the state park.

When I arrived, the tide was out and the sky was cloudless. A few sea-smoothed boulders of ancient rock stuck out of powdery, yellow sand. The ocean was calm by Cape standards, a sheet of gently swelling white light. I remembered my family coming here before Aggie disappeared.

The distant whine of a motorboat engine sounded on the water. A battered fishing trawler, with a winch and a crane on the back, made its way to a concrete jetty at the water's edge. Elliott raised a hand from the wheelhouse.

I walked over.

"Didn't know you fished."

Elliott held out his hand and helped me in.

"My old man's boat. There's something I need to show you."

I sat beside Elliott in the wheelhouse. Time-weathered cliffs and tide pools went past. The rocks on the East Cape were inaccessible from the land, lending things a forlorn air.

Elliott dropped anchor and pointed to a dark semicircle in the bottom of the cliffs.

"That's where we're going."

He dropped a kayak into the water. We stripped to our wetsuits and climbed in. He handed me an oar.

We rowed to the jagged mouth in the rocks. There was just enough room for us to bend forward and row into a gloomy, elongated basin of slopping sea water. Above us, a high ceiling disappeared into an impenetrable shadow.

We got out onto a thin strip of sandy beach.

"How d'you know about this place?" I said.

Elliott cracked a glow stick and held it up.

"I do trips for kids I teach."

Ahead of us, a curious wooden ship bobbed up and down in the water, nudging against the sides of the cave.

"It looks like a pirate ship," I said.

"It's an old sloop, more than a hundred feet long. From the early nineteenth century, I think."

The ship's figurehead was a cat's head with a snake's body.

"How did it get in here?" I said. "Could it have washed up in the storm?"

"No. It's way too big. And there's something else that doesn't make sense - this is a sailing ship but there are no masts or sails."

From where we stood, the age-blackened hull was too high above the water to see the boat's deck.

We dived into the dark water and swam over. The boat gave off an aroma of rotten meat, sweetened by a sickly perfume.

"How do we get onboard?" I said.

Elliott held up a coil of nylon rope with a black grappling hook on one end.

"I came prepared this time."

He swung it a few times and let go. The hook sailed into the air, dropping into the boat with a thud.

I followed him up the rope and grabbed onto a wooden rail at the top. A piece came off in my hands. I rolled down the hull's side into Elliot's arms.

There is a kind of electric charge sometimes, isn't there?

"Are you going to put me down?"

He dropped me onto the wooden deck, which stood about half way up the hull. We walked over to a pile of ancient wooden crates in the middle of the boat. Elliott took out a clasp knife and pried one open. It was full of giant ostrich eggs, wrapped in straw and sawdust.

I opened up an aging, leather chest beside it. There were rolls of copper coins wrapped in twists of decayed paper. I took a coin out. It was smooth on both sides.

"Borrow pence," I said.

"What?"

"Cape name for old coins. Worn smooth. Never actually seen one before."

A long bench at the stern was covered with iron collars and ankle chains.

"Slaves," Elliott said.

A carefully stacked pile of triangular bars, dark and waxy, stood at the prow of the ship. Elliott picked one up and smelt it.

"Beeswax. Very old."

The missing bar revealed something metal underneath. We pulled bars away until the top of a steel drum was revealed.

"Mark 77," I said. "Incendiary fluid. Ex-military. More than enough to get this boat impounded. I'll phone the Sheriff's Marine Patrol. Ham Rourke can be here in half an hour. He can deal with Homeland or the F.B.I. or the army."

Elliott shook his head.

"I can't be tangled up in any of this," he said. "I don't trust the authorities here, no offense."

I thought for a moment and nodded.

"Okay. I'll say I got an anonymous tip-off."

We dived off the old boat. As we boarded the kayak, Elliott wedged something into a shadowy gap in the rock.

"Video camera," he said.

When we were on board the Mud Hen, I sat on the wheelhouse passenger seat. Elliott rubbed his chin and pointed at the shore.

"The proposed marine sanctuary is on this stretch of coast."

"Yeah. Up to Narwak."

"What's happening here happened before. The native tribes suffered a catastrophe when the colonists arrived. It took a while. First smallpox, then gold miners polluted the rivers with chemicals. Starvation followed, federal de-recognition and finally deportation. The Cape had plentiful salmon, mussel beds, deer, and elk. It provided for everyone."

"Andy Rheinholdz thought someone was deliberately running Cape Misfortune down," I said.

Elliott nodded.

"I met Andy on a joint operation with the Coast Guard. Good guy. Like I said, I don't think any of the people killed by Henderson that day were a coincidence. Andy was sniffing around. The bank teller was a critic of the pipeline. Even the bank security guy was a fisherman who protested about river pollution."

"What about you?"

"I started a petition supporting the Reserve."

"There's no evidence. This could all be put down to coincidence."

Elliott shrugged.

"There are too many co-incidences around here."

I looked out at the ocean, which was reflecting the dark blue sky, and told Elliott everything. Charlie; the cattle mutilation maps; even the astral traveling. His dark eyes never once left my face. When I finished, he laughed.

"Wow."

"Are the Islands of the Dead mentioned in local, Native American belief?"

He shook his head.

"Not that I know of. Wish Bay enjoys a bit of a reputation for strange things washing up, but this is European. Something they brought with them."

"Do you think I'm crazy?"

He put his hand on my shoulder.

"The flying fog man on the rooftop rescued me as well, remember? I've never doubted you."

We hugged and, truth be told, it didn't feel that awkward.

He started the Mud Hen's engine.

"After the fog-man got us off the roof, Wilson Paderborn came for me, and Cath Claybourne, for you."

"These are ruthless people."

"We need to be careful. Let's try and make sure it isn't the third time lucky."

Chapter Nineteen
Ellen and Roy

I called Ham Rourke. Then I tracked Charlie down to a high dependency ward in Venice City hospital. He was breathing through a ventilator surrounded by a circle of machines.

An old couple, sitting by his bed, turned to look at me.

The man's eyes looked shrewd and unforgiving. A shock of dirty, grey hair hung out from underneath an old, Valkyrie Wolves baseball cap.

"Are you Charlie's parents?" I asked.

"Oh, no," the woman answered. "Charlie's parents are estranged from him. We're Patrick's parents."

She was slightly built and had prominent cheek bones.

"I'm Cassie, a friend of Charlie."

"I'm Ellen, and this is Roy," the woman said, gesturing to the man.

"Doctors say anything?" I asked.

"Only that he's unresponsive. They're investigating. They don't know why."

Charlie made a loud grunt of pain.

"He does that now and then. How'd you know our Charlie?" Roy said.

"We met a few days ago."

"Did I hear you were up at the old Wessendorf house with him?" Ellen asked.

"No. Who told you that?"

"Heard it on the grapevine. Best to stay away from places like that," Ellen said.

She smiled. Roy sighed, and sprinkled a line of tobacco into a cigarette paper.

"They used to have ashtrays beside the bed in hospitals. Everything is so politically correct nowadays."

A nurse came in.

"Visiting time is over. We have more tests to run."

Charlie made another pained grunt.

"I wish we'd never come to Cape Misfortune. The place is cursed," Helen said, as we walked out. "The clue is in the name."

There was another storm that night. I dreamt Charlie was fighting for something, not just his life. I was woken when hailstones as big as fists knocked my tent down. I got hit on my hand as I ran to the back porch. The bogs carried a faint, rank smell of death but, for once, I had no ghostly visitors.

I woke in the rocking chair. The tall weeds on the lawn were all flattened. On the bright side, the new roof had once again triumphed.

"Dispatch just took a 911. Missing juvenile," Ann said, as I got to Needle Point." Lake Slaughter psychiatric unit. I don't want you involved."

"Why not?"

Ann looked at me.

"All right. Do you think your sister is dead?"

I didn't blink.

"Yes. So, do I take the call or not?"

She hesitated.

"If it's an abduction, it will most likely get kicked up to state or federal anyway."

I drove to the lake.

As I walked up the familiar corridors, a young patient named Trent came out of his room.

"Hey, Cassie, what's with the Halloween costume?"

"I've re-integrated into the community," I said,

Nurse Hopkins sat at the nurse's station. When she saw me her lips curled into a sneer.

"I'm here about a report of a missing person," I said.

"You were called out for nothing. The individual who made the call is having a bad day."

"Can I speak with her?"

"Absolutely not. Seeing a uniformed police officer is the last thing she needs."

"Do you have an on-duty doctor I can talk to?"

"It wouldn't make any difference."

Boone walked up the corridor. Hopkins stood up, smiling.

"Deputy Washienko, welcome. I'm afraid there has been a big mistake."

"Is that right?" Boone asked.

"A patient remembered her daughter who died two years ago today. Anniversaries can be upsetting. She gets confused, poor thing. She got past security and used the old, public phone by the lake."

Two orderlies dragged a struggling woman up the corridor. Her hair was disheveled and her bathrobe dirty.

"What's your name, ma'am?" I asked.

"Grace Hamrick."

"What's going on, Grace?"

"My daughter Sasha was taken last night."

"You see who took her?" Boone said.

"That's enough. You're encouraging her delusions," Nurse Hopkins said.

"A man who smelt bad took my little girl," Grace said.

"You know his name?" I said.

"Eugene. He was working for Julius Wessendorf. They all are, Hopkins included."

"Enough!" Hopkins said. "Get her to the ICU."

They dragged Grace Hamrick towards the room of Joachim Alvarez's murder. Hopkins placed a syringe and an ampoule of Vacuphase on a cardboard tray. Her hand shook.

"They took my mom too, in the early nineties. Her name was Clara Albrecht!" Hamrick shouted.

Boone put his hand on my shoulder.

"Come on, Cass."

"I will make a formal complaint about you badgering sick and vulnerable patients," Hopkins said.

Out in the parking lot, Boone shook his head.

"I always wonder if you're crazy or brave."

"Brave? I ran away on the Kommerz bank roof."

He looked down at his feet. When he looked up, his eyes were moist.

"We both know that didn't happen."

"Well, isn't this nice, just like the end of a John Wayne movie," a British voice said.

Dame Teddy strode towards us, wearing a white lab coat over horse-riding gear.

"Deputy Washienko, when you've finished blubbing, I need a word with your ex-wife," she said, walking past us.

"You know where I am, Cass," Boone said.

I followed Teddy down an unfamiliar corridor into a square treatment room with a central dentist-style chair in the middle. She sat back on it with her hands behind her head.

"Old Sparky, we call this. You heard of electroconvulsive therapy?"

"What do you want?"

She held up a chocolate lolly.

"Want one? I give them to the children, but only if they've been good."

"I'll pass."

Teddy put it in her mouth and sucked it.

"What do you really want from life, Cassandra?"

"My sister back. My father, too. And maybe Grace Hamrick's daughter."

She tutted.

"You are proving resistant to treatment, sweet one. Dad and sis are long gone. Dead as dodos. Poor Grace Hamrick's darling little daughter is worm food."

"I don't think that's true."

"I have a picture in my head. A charming scene of you and Boone on a sweet, little cranberry farm raising a host of darling brats."

She chewed the lolly.

"Another picture. You carry on being naughty and end up strapped to this electric chair. Plugged into the mains until you can't remember what your damn name is. A nappy woman!"

Teddy threw back her head and laughed at that, kicking her feet in the air.

"Because this room is where it could all end up if you're a naughty girl, Cassie. Now get out before I press my panic button and get you injected with something powerful."

"They would be assaulting a police officer."

"Ooh, fancy Dan. I should never have let you out," Teddy shouted, through the door as I left.

Chapter Twenty
Handsome Hank

I sat in the hospital parking lot searching through missing juveniles on the mobile computer. The county had forty-nine open cases, but there was no mention of Hamrick's mother, Clara Albrecht.

I drove to the Sheriff's Headquarters in Valkyrie to check on anything made before things went digital.

The HQ had once been a library. Tall windows stood between ornate pillars topped with the carved faces of the town's founding fathers.

The Investigation Division was in an oval-shaped office that took up the first floor. I recognized a few of the faces looking up from behind computer monitors. I was unpopular for shooting Cath, so faces hardened when they saw me.

The basement was a vast, dimly-lit, warren of metal shelves scented with the sweet and sour aroma of decaying paper and dust. Two minutes into my search, I realized the boxes I wanted were gone. There were cleaner, box-sized marks in the dust where they should have been.

I heard footsteps behind me.

"Shouldn't you be out on patrol or something?" a deep voice said.

I turned. Hank Frederson stood behind me, crisply turned out in a blue Captain's uniform, a look of wintry dislike on his sun-tanned face.

"Following a lead on a case, sir."

"You know, I liked life before computers. Things were simpler. Now any idiot can read about any damn thing. May I enquire what your investigation is about?"

"Missing juvenile, sir."

"Why haven't I heard about this? I'm not aware of any active investigations."

"I only took the call this morning."

Hank stuck his hands in his pockets and leaned forward.

"I understand that was a false alarm from a vulnerable, psychiatric patient. So why are you wasting time, down in this old basement, on a crime that didn't happen?"

"I thought I'd read up on some background. It's my lunch break, sir."

"Lunch? It's not even eleven o'clock."

"I'm taking it early, sir."

"Where is it?"

"What?"

"Your lunch?"

"I've eaten it."

He sucked in a cheek and bit on it. Then he walked over until he was so close I could smell citrus deodorant.

"You grew up on the Cape, did you not?"

"Born and bred, sir."

He grabbed the collars of my duty jacket and pushed me against the shelves.

"Then why are you such a stupid, interfering bitch? You should know from your idiot father what happens to troublemakers."

I grabbed his wrists and pushed him away.

"Are you in on this, Hank?" I said.

"In on what?"

"This whole thing."

"Teddy seems to like you. I don't. You're not a team player. You have no respect for your senior officers, or this department."

With that he walked off, stopping to flip the bird from halfway down the corridor.

Ham Rourke called me as I climbed into the patrol car.

"Cave was empty, Cass. No boat."

"Okay. Sorry to send you on a wild goose chase, Ham."

"Hey, this is Cape Misfortune."

Later, on my real lunch break, a web search turned up an old story, in the Cape Misfortune Sentinel, on Grace Hamrick's mother.

"Bingo."

Clara Albrecht had disappeared while riding her horse on the beach. Her daughter, Grace Hamrick, then a toddler, told an unlikely story about a fat man putting her mother in a slave wagon. Grace was taken into care.

The piece ended with an appeal for information by Deputy Buzz Everett. The by-line was for a reporter called Caroline Severin who now worked for Venice TV, presenting the local news. I found a clip of her on YouTube.

It began with Dame Teddy Champion walking on the Valkyrie waterfront, looking small but jaunty beside Caroline Severin, a tall blonde in her late fifties who wore salmon-pink lipstick.

"It has been called the Pacific Northwest's Bermuda Triangle. The recent disappearance of a fishing boat with a three man crew the latest in a series of mysterious disappearances on the rocky headland that is officially the foggiest place in America," Severin said. "But, there may now be a rational explanation for Cape Misfortune's disappearances. I'm here with Dame Professor Edwina Champion."

"It's the sort of mass hysteria outbreak that sometimes happens in modern society," Teddy said. "I tell all the Cape people that blaming the disappearances on any, single factor is utter nonsense. And, you know what? They get terribly cross with me."

Teddy giggled, mischievously.

"Well, I'm feeling a little less hysterical already," Severin said.

The clip ended.

An hour later, I walked through the offices of Venice TV. Caroline Severin looked out of a door. She ushered me into a small office and held out her hand.

"How can I help you, Deputy?"

She wore a smart business suit that looked expensive.

"While you were at the Sentinel, you reported on the abduction of a young mother named Clara Albrecht."

Her smile faded.

"That was a very long time ago."

"Her granddaughter was recently reported missing."

She examined her shoes.

"I don't do abduction stories anymore. And I don't want to talk to you."

She looked around the office.

"Are you anything to do with Charlie Playfair?"

"Why would you say that?"

"He came here asking questions. I'll tell you what I told him. When I reported on the cattle mutilations, I was driven off the road one night. My soul flew across the ocean to a stone island with a dead tree. I think it was the Isle of the Dead. I woke hanging upside down in my car. I never want to go back there."

"Quite a story."

Her blue eyes were moist.

"You have to ask yourself. Is what's happening on Cape Misfortune worth dying for? Or worse than dying? I have a nice house now. My children go to a good school."

"People are being abducted. They may come for your children one day."

"My advice to you? Get a different job. Move out of state. And Deputy…"

"Yeah?"
"Don't ever contact me again."

Chapter Twenty-One
All Aboard

In the afternoon, Elliot texted me to meet him on some Shell tribal land east of Venice.

I drove down unfamiliar country roads. The tribe was given a few thousand acres of forest in 1998, parceled out along the Shell River.

I parked in a muddy forest clearing. The fir trees were tall and the forest canopy closed-up, making things feel confined.

Elliott was not here.

I heard a chainsaw in the distance.

I was getting ready to go when there was a scream that suddenly cut off. I ran towards the source until I came to a clearing.

There was an old oak tree in the middle of a forest pasture. Elliott hung by his neck from a high branch. His face was swollen. He looked down at me and kicked his legs.

Two figures ran out of the clearing, rustling through the ferns.

Elliott was too high up for me to get his legs. The rope was tethered to the tree trunk. I took a multi-tool from my gear belt and sawed. It took longer than I wanted. The cord finally gave. Elliott fell to the forest floor.

It took a second to get my fingers under the hangman's knot so I could loosen it.

He lay on his back, breath going in and out in a wheezing whistle. After sucking in air for a while, he sat up and spat out watery blood.

"Thanks for saving my life. Again. Can you get these off?"

He turned. I cut a plastic tie around his wrists.

"Did you get a look at them?"

"One was a dead ringer for Cath Claybourn. Except she's dead, isn't she?"

"Who was the other one?"

"White male, fifties. Smelled of meat."

"Biker's vest?"

"Yeah. You know him?"

"Our paths have crossed."

Elliott fingered a bright red line around his neck.

"Whoever it was, they were strong. I couldn't get them off me."

"I should call this in," I said.

He held up a hand.

"They'll say I did it to myself. Probably send me to see your friend, Dame Teddy."

Elliott asked to be dropped off at a local gas station.

As I drove to Venice hospital, a newscaster announced Hank Frederson had won the election for Sheriff of Venice County.

I saw something in the marshes, stopped my car and got out. The afternoon sun picked out the outline of wheel tracks among tufts of grass and mud. The sort left by an old wagon.

At the hospital, a silver-haired man in surgical scrubs talked to Roy and Ellen. His expression was grave.

"They're thinking about moving things on," Roy said.

Ellen nodded gravely.

"Charlie's brain function is deteriorating. Put simply; any recovery is doubtful," the doctor said.

"I need more time," I said.

They stared at me uncomprehendingly. The doctor shook his head.

"This is a medical decision. It's cruel to prolong his life."

I sat with Charlie's body for a while and then went home. My kitchen now had a cooker and fridge, all plumbed in. I saw Charlie's name flash up on my cell.

"It's Roy, Patrick's father. I need to talk."

"Roy, it's late, I've had a long day."

"Meet me at the old Wessendorf house. There's a fog coming, so hurry."

"The house fell over a cliff."

"Just come."

I met Roy beneath what remained of the boundary wall. He wore a camouflage coat. A hunting rifle was slung over his shoulder.

"You expecting trouble?" I said.

"Are you kidding? This is Cape Misfortune."

I took him to the collapsed wall. We climbed into what remained of the garden.

The storm had dragged most of the hill including Julius's domed tomb and the entire mausoleum, into the ocean, leaving a fresh cliff edge, jagged and dark.

Only the old house's eastern tower had survived. It now looked like the chess piece on the tapestry.

"This is where we'll camp," Roy said. "We'll get a good view."

"We're near the edge. It doesn't look safe."

"Nothing in life is."

He opened a window. Inside there was a cast-iron stove, and a row of kitchen closets ranged around a curved wall. Metal pots and pans littered the brick floor. The back wall had fallen over the cliff, offering a view of Wish Bay.

Roy rolled himself a cigarette.

"Smoking will give our position away," I said.

He lit the cigarette and inhaled.

"Everything is so politically correct. Don't do this, don't do that."

"Roy, what are we doing out here?"

He took a silver, hip flask from his pocket.

"Fancy a nip?"

I shook my head.

"Children go missing from the Cape every generation," Roy said. "There are plenty of theories about why."

"You have one?"

Roy took a sip.

"Oh, yeah. They're sacrificed."

"To who?"

Roy shrugged.

"Who knows? The early settlers made a pact with someone - or something."

"Interesting theory. One thing I've never understood is how something this big can be hushed up."

"Power can do anything it wants. You learn that as you get older."

As he spoke a new fog appeared in Wish Bay, oozing across the ocean.

"You can't beat the otherworld, Cassie. It's like going up against a country. They keep coming for you."

"Who does?"

Roy shaped his mouth into an 'O' and blew a smoke ring that drifted out of the window.

"Creatures every bit as smart and stubborn as you are my dear, and much more powerful."

He looked at the luminous dials of his watch.

"You heard of the Marsh witches?"

"Everyone has."

"Here's the truth. In the old days of Cape Misfortune, before the law came, when people started going missing, they needed someone to blame. They blamed the Indians at first and hung a fair few of them. But that theory didn't hold water because it carried on after they were kicked out."

Roy laughed. It turned into a wheezing cackle. Outside a tendril of advancing fog began to lick the remaining garden.

"So, they started blaming witches. And by witches, that meant anyone who wasn't a fan of young Julius Wessendorf."

A faint sound came out of Wish Bay. *Clickety-clack.* Roy crushed his cigarette on the floor.

"You know Seven Mile Lane started as Julius's private train track? Why not? He was a millionaire. There was only ever one railroad car, with silk padding on the inside and blacked-out windows."

"If I remember my history, all the railroad tracks were ripped up soon after the motor car arrived."

The *clickety-clack* noise was joined by the unmistakeable *huff-puff* sound of a steam engine.

I looked out of the window. Half a mile away, high above Wish Bay, on ghostly land long ago taken by storms, a steam locomotive rode over opaque rail tracks.

A rifle barrel stuck in my back.

"I gave them my son Patrick, as a sacrifice. I worked hard to give him a good life, but he was a disappointment to me, so it didn't hurt too badly. I do the odd job for them now and then. You must have really pissed someone off, Cassie."

A hundred feet beyond the cliff edge, a ghostly brick platform formed out of the fog.

"What do you get in return, Roy?"

"Eternal life."

The locomotive pulled in to the fog station. A whistle sounded. The passenger car door opened. Cath Claybourn jumped down onto the ghost platform and shook her wings. She wore a freshly-pressed, Venice County uniform now. There was a row of medals. Her eyes turned towards me. She held up her hand and made a goofy face while jingling some slave chains.

"Those are for you, I'm afraid," Roy said.

I saw Nurse Trudy Hopkins emerge from the shadows of the last, remaining, hawthorn tree. A four year old girl held her hand. Sasha Hamrick, I guessed, the child Hopkins told me was two years dead.

"You've been outmaneuvered, Deputy," Roy said. "You never stood a chance. Let this be your final life lesson."

Cath flew up the garden towards us. I wondered if Aggie had ridden this train. Roy pressed the rifle in my back.

"You are going to get on the choo-choo. Don't try anything. Dead, or alive, it's all one to me. Move."

I climbed through the window but, as I dropped to the floor, I rolled across the paving stones into the thick fog.

"You stupid bitch!" Roy shouted, firing his rifle.

I heard it go past my ear and hit the paving stone beside me. In the darkness, I felt something metal. An old saucepan. I ran up to beside the window and flattened myself against the wall. Roy jumped out. I swung where I thought his head would be. My improvised weapon connected and he fell. I scooped his rifle up and ran towards the train.

Hopkins was somehow standing on the ghost platform, encouraging the Hamrick girl to get onto the metal step below the passenger car door.

I heard wings beating overhead and squinted through the rifle's telescopic sights. Cath looked down at me. I fired. She fell out of the sky.

The uniformed, engine driver opened a door and looked out. He wore a peaked cap and had mutton-chop sideburns. His eyes were pools of darkness. He went back in.

The locomotive started to pull out. I ran down to the cliff edge. Sasha Hamrick stared at me through a half-opened window in the passenger car. Cath flew over me, her path twisting and erratic, before she thumped onto the engine car roof and lay still. I tried to get my foot onto the ghost platform but it plunged into nothing. I saw Sasha's terrified face and cried out in frustration.

Wessendorf's private train disappeared into the fog above Wish Bay. The noise died to a faint *clickety-clack* and then it was gone.

A cold wind blew the fog away. I heard wheezing behind me. Roy hobbled over. His face was smeared with blood.

"You're such an old-fashioned stand-up guy, Roy, selling children into slavery," I said.

"My deal was to hand you over."

"Hand me over to who?"

"I think you broke my nose."

"Who are you working for?"

"No chance. You'd have to kill me."

"Don't tempt me."

I pushed him through the breached wall.

"I'm friendly with Hank Frederson," he said.

"I'll bet you are."

When we got to my truck, Roy chuckled.

"Don't bother telling folks about our adventure tonight. Mental patients with wild stories of ghost trains don't get taken too seriously."

"Just for that, Roy, you can walk home."

Chapter Twenty-Two
Stripes

Someone knocked on my new front door. Boone stood outside. His pale, handsome face was full of remorse.

"I've had a really long day," I said.

"I've been worried about you. Thought maybe we could go for a drink. I'm buying."

"I want to ask you a question, Boone. It was a hopeless situation on the bank roof. I get that. You panicked and left everyone for dead. That, I also understand. But why let me swing in the wind afterward? People said I fled the crime scene. It's a miracle I kept my job."

He looked down at his feet.

"I panicked. I was afraid of people knowing I was a chicken. You were a witness. I'll spend the rest of my life making it up to you."

I had a non-alcoholic drink with him in Venice. Then I drove home.

That night, I slept in my old bedroom. The only ghosts were those of imagination and memory.

In the morning, I enjoyed my first hot shower in the restored bathroom.

Kurt Deakins had bought me a coffee machine. I made a cup and sat on the porch working out my story for when Roy inevitably caused trouble.

At Needlepoint, Ann did not look up from her computer screen.

"Just reading through your crime reports. I've never known a Venice County officer who gets in as many scrapes as you do."

"If you are going to tear a stripe off me, can you do it quickly? I'd like to get out on patrol."

Ann leaned back in her chair and chuckled.

"Sheriff-elect Frederson phoned me this morning. He wants you fired."

"What for?"

"He said you roughed up a good buddy of his, Roy Feuer."

"Roy took a shot at me with a hunting rifle."

Ann shook her head.

"Hank also claimed you bothered vulnerable patients at the psychiatric hospital."

I unpinned the tin star from my shirt and tossed it onto her desk.

"You always believe everyone but me."

"You didn't let me finish what I was saying."

"I don't have to listen to your lectures anymore."

I walked to the door.

"Wait."

Ann picked the star up.

"Frederson is a creep. He was a creep when I worked with him as a young deputy, and he still is now. He's the subject of a clandestine investigation by Douglas County detectives – at the request of Sheriff Fairhurst. It seems Hank took money from the gas pipe people, amongst others."

Ann threw the badge at me. I caught it, reflexively.

She opened her desk drawer.

"I hope you can sew."

She handed me a badge with two V-shaped stripes on it.

"I don't understand."

"I'm promoting you to corporal."

"Why?"

She walked around her desk and held out both her hands. I took them.

"This morning, Boone Washienko came by. He changed his statement about what happened at the bank. Seems you didn't flee. It's made me re-think everything you've done. Seems I've been very, very wrong about you, Cassie. You showed strength of character on the roof, then in the way you handled the shooter at Valkyrie High and later, I now realize, with Cath. I didn't realize you were one of the good guys. And for that, I'm very sorry."

"There's a lot of bad stuff going on around here," I said.

"And you've been doing your best to stop it. Have a good shift, Corporal."

She winked.

My first job as a newly-promoted peace officer was for a 'man down' outside a carpet store showroom, in a business park north of Valkyrie. Billy Teutoberger, a large man, late middle-age, lay on the sidewalk. His eyes were open but non-responsive. A young woman knelt beside him.

"Is he on anything?" I said.

"This isn't drugs. Look at his hand."

There was a curved blade in his palm.

I knelt and took his pulse. It was light and erratic.

"Seen the knife before?" I asked.

"No. I know what it is, though. I've never seen anyone stupid enough to pick one up before."

A guy from the Cape should know a geschank when he sees one, I thought.

An orange and white Venice County ambulance pulled up. I stepped back to let the EMTs do their work. They loaded Ulrich on a stretcher and drove off.

I scooped the knife into the bag without holding it.

"You picked it up?" the woman asked.

"He already touched it. The curse only works once."

"Maybe. You want my advice? Throw it out of the window when you are in the marshes. Into water."

Chapter Twenty-Three
The Love Triangle

In the evening, I drove my truck to Ukobach beach. The sun was a low ball of flame, coloring the surf a deep red-orange.

Three teenagers sat on the sand smoking dope.

"You should bust those kids," a voice behind me said.

I turned to see Boone.

"What are you doing here?"

"Oh, I was just on the beach and...okay, I'm stalking you."

"I'm busy. I'm meeting someone."

"I'm suspended."

"I heard."

"I just want to know that we're okay."

He held out his grandmother's wedding ring.

"Boone, you have got to be kidding me."

"Not to get married again. I just want you to have it."

"I needed it when you took it off me in the psychiatric unit."

I looked around. The Mud Hen was docking at the concrete jetty with the shadow of Elliott in the cockpit.

"I've got to go."

Boone followed me up the jetty.

"I have news about Bliss Schneider," he said.

"Can it wait?"

When we got to the boat, Elliott stepped out of the wheelhouse.

"I don't mean to be rude, but you're not welcome, Deputy Washienko."

"I have news about Bliss."

Elliott thought about that and stepped back. Boone got in.

"I think Miss Schneider helped commission acts of terrorism," Boone said, once Elliott had fired up the engine, and we started moving. "I followed her a couple of times. She made a cash drop-off in a trash can outside Venice City."

"Who picked it up?" I said.

"Middle-aged guy. Military-looking. The license plate on the car was from out-of-state. Leased by Coffi."

"You follow him?"

"He took a boat to Narwak lighthouse."

"When was this?"

"About a week ago."

"Why didn't you tell anyone?" I said.

Boone shrugged. Elliott smiled.

"I knew Schneider was involved."

We rowed to the cave. Boone swam behind the kayak in his boxers.

The camera was where Elliott had hidden it.

"What are we looking for?" Boone said.

"Not sure," Elliott said.

We dived into dark water and shone our lights on a sandy bed. Faceless coins lay strewn around an ancient-looking, silver geschank, which was buried in the sand, ivory handle upwards. To my horror, Boone pulled it out. I shook it out of his hand and we swam to the surface.

"What's the problem?" Boone said.

"You never heard of a geschank?"

Back on the boat, Boone started to shiver so badly Elliott put a blanket over his shoulders.

"I'm from Venice City, the mainland," Boone said, his teeth chattering. "I've never heard of a ge-whatever-it-is."

The last red light of the sunset made him look as if he was already in hell.

"I'm not a total skeptic about stuff," he said. "I can call the rain."

Elliott smiled.

"You mean like a shaman?"

"I learned on a summer camp once. A Native American song. More of a chant."

"What tradition is it a part of?" Elliot asked.

"I don't know."

"How much rain can you call?"

"Depends. Could be a big storm, could be a light shower."

"How fast can you bring it?"

"There's the rub. It can take anything from a few seconds to a couple of days."

Elliott laughed.

"That's not a great achievement. It rains all the time on this rock."

"Funny thing. It only ever works on the Cape."

Boone stood up and sang. It was a mournful melody with words I didn't understand, but clear and pure, resonating in the darkening, evening water.

Elliott put a hand on my ex-husband's shoulder.

"That was beautiful," he said.

Black storm clouds appeared on the horizon. Elliott gunned the engines. There was an answering rumble of thunder. In a few minutes, clouds rolled overhead. The rain fell so hard, we couldn't see beyond the edge of the boat.

"I'm sorry, Cass," Boone said, his teeth chattering.

He held out his grandmother's ring. Seeing it was like a cloud moving over the sun. His betrayal had been so complete.

"We're divorced. You dumped me."

But I took it because I was starting to feel sorry for him.

By the time we got to the beach, the rain clouds had cleared. Boone was shaking. He jumped onto the jetty and waved a hand.

"You going to be okay?" I asked.

"Yeah. I'll see you fellas around?"

We watched him disappear into the trees beyond the beach.

"You believe in the geschank stuff?" Elliot asked.

"Why not? We just watched a guy call the rain."

I drove along winding back roads to Elliott's house on the western coast. It was an old fisherman's cottage with thick, stone walls overlooking a rocky cove.

Elliott arrived a few minutes later and moored his boat.

"I'm hungry. Do you want something to eat?"

"Can you cook?"

"I make a few signature dishes," Elliott said, with a smile.

"Maybe later."

Inside, it was sparse but comfortable. An old sofa and some wooden chairs stood around a little, log-burning stove.

"I grew up here," Elliott said.

We sat at a dining table. I watched the dark ocean through a window, while he plugged the portable camera into a computer. A video feed of the cave appeared on the screen. The wooden boat bobbed up and down in the background. The time code said 4:18 pm.

Nothing happened. Elliott fast forwarded. At 3:06 in the morning, tendrils of fog crept through the cave mouth.

"Does this have sound?" I asked.

Elliott turned the volume up.

There was a long sound, like a moan. Fog filled the cave. The old boat glowed.

Then all of the wooden planks on the boat's hull buckled, splintered and broke with a noise like a box of firecrackers going off. Fleshy pulp oozed out of the cracked wood, pink and crimson, twisting into smooth intestines that curled around each other, before forming into a hard oval sitting on the water. Then the egg started to crack. Sharp talons emerged, followed by a curved beak and wings. From the long span, it looked like a bird of prey. The creature beat its wings and hovered over the cave water. Then it dived into the dark water with a splash. Elliott fast-forwarded until the fog cleared. The cave was empty.

"We should show this to Ham," I said.

Elliott shook his head.

"He won't believe this. No one will. They'll think we photoshopped it."

"I'm going to go and check on Boone," I said.

We both looked out to sea. There was a dirty line of fog creeping over the night-time water.

"I'll tag along," Elliot said.

Chapter Twenty-Four
Snatched

Thick fog kept pace with my truck as we tore through Valkyrie's winding streets.

"My Dad told us the brain could get confused by patterns in the fog; see things that aren't there. Patterns that resemble an animal, a bird, or even a person".

"This goes way beyond that," Elliott said.

"You saw the fog man, the people who tried to lynch you, didn't you?"

"I did."

"I doubt myself, even though I have such clear memories – flying over the Hiddensee with Charlie, Agata on the rocks, the slave wagon, Wessendorf's train, Andi Malone's murder."

"I believe you," Elliott said.

My former married home was a second floor apartment in a leafy, Valkyrie neighborhood.

"You been back here since the divorce?" Elliot asked.

"Why would I?"

The place was like a knife wound.

The light flickered out of Boone's window as if someone was watching television in the dark.

I pressed the intercom.

"Boone?"

A young woman burst out of the front door. Long dark hair obscured her face. She tried to get past but I grabbed her.

"What's going on up there?" I said.

Her body trembled. Dark, stricken eyes stared back at me.

"You're the wife."

"Ex-wife. Who are you?"

She pushed me away.

"Ex-girlfriend."

"Is Boone up there?"

But she disappeared into the fog. We went up the stairs. Light spilled from the crack beneath the apartment door. There was noise, too - a crackling sound, like a cliff collapsing, followed by grunts of pain and glass breaking.

Elliott pushed the door. The room was bathed in a white glow. Which was odd, because the lights were all off.

A rippling circle of darkness hung in the air where an old fireplace usually stood. The back wheels of the slave wagon stood on the carpet. The cage door on the vehicle's back was open.

Boone was in the middle of the room swinging his fists around. His eyes were closed. His nose was bloody. A fat man in a biker's leather vest laughed and dodged his blows.

I went into our old bedroom. Boone's gear belt lay on top of his discarded uniform, as it always did. I picked up his radio and gave the code for officer needs assistance.

I went back into a wall of freezing air. The front room was gone. A dead tree stood on a plateau of rock on a high cliff. Icebergs floated in the sea far below, looking like frozen beasts.

Biker's vest was heaving an unconscious Boone into the wagon.

"Hey, sweetcheeks," he said. "Room for two in here."

His upper lip was coated with a film of luminous sweat.

I grabbed his arm.

"You're under arrest," I said.

The fat man hit me on the nose with the flat of his palm. My eyes went out of focus. I fell backward onto the rocks.

"Why are you doing this?" I asked.

He sighed.

"Because a human being is a very precious thing. Worth more than money."

Elliott appeared from behind the tree. His lower lip was split open. He staggered forwards and wrapped himself around biker's vest's knees.

A distant police siren sounded from another world. Biker's vest kicked Elliott off and climbed into the driver's seat.

For a second, I saw the wagon on an icy road. Then the room's walls solidified out of gathering mist. The rippling hole in the wall shrank into nothing. Elliott sat up and wiped the blood from his lip.

"Poor Boone," I said.

"Yeah."

We gave edited statements to the Valkyrie cops in the corridor outside Boone's apartment, while the forensic team worked inside.

They cut Elliott loose after a couple of hours.

Ulrich Honeyglass said Boone's girlfriend was called Paris Geil. It turned out she was a DUI arrest he made. Unprofessional, I thought, although that was now the least of his problems.

Sheriff Fairhurst turned up. He squeezed my shoulder like we were old friends.

"Take a walk?"

We strolled down to the river. The fog was gone, and the neighborhood was asleep. Boone and I often made this walk.

I stood on the bank with Hilly and watched the water glisten in the moonlight.

The Sheriff stroked his white beard.

"You're from the Cape?"

"Yes, sir."

He smiled.

"Let's take the old superstitions as read, then. I can understand a hungry tatzelwurm coming out of the fog, hunting for fresh meat, but why would anyone want to steal people?"

I shrugged.

"Tell me straight, what happened in that room?"

I saw some tiny cracks of moonlight between the trees on the opposite bank.

"Boone was abducted by a slave wagon from across the Hiddensee."

Hilly whistled.

"Deep Cape"

"Captain Frederson is involved somehow. And Dame Teddy Champion."

"The British shrink, how so?"

"She's recruiting vulnerable patients."

"For what?"

"I think something big is going to happen. On Walpurgisnacht."

"The night before my rival takes over."

"I think they are going to try and set fire to the state park, maybe the whole Cape."

"Any reason you think that?"

"I've discovered illegal barrels of a military incendiary gel called Mark 77 during my investigations."

"Why haven't I heard about this?"

"They were stolen."

Hilly shook his head.

"I looked the other way too many times. How I have failed our beloved rock."

Chapter Twenty-Five
The Tunnel of God

"Mr. Playfair was taken off a respirator at eight-thirty this morning. He died, peacefully, a few minutes later. I'm sorry."

The young nurse didn't look sorry. His face said I was a troublemaker.

"Who made the decision?" I said.

"A senior consultant, after speaking to Mr. and Mrs. Feuer."

"The Feuers aren't next of kin. They're the parents of his missing partner."

"I wouldn't know about that."

"Who was the consultant?"

"A senior neuro-psychiatrist familiar with the case."

"Dame Teddy Champion?" I said.

The nurse nodded.

I walked to the hospital morgue, in the early morning sunshine, and told the attendant I was working on a case involving Charlie. She was a friendly, short-haired woman in her early sixties. After consulting with her computer, she opened up a metal drawer.

The body had gone. She tried a few more drawers.

"He has to be around here somewhere," she said.

Dan called me as I got into the patrol car.

"Thought you might want a heads up. Early forensics just came through. Fingerprints at the crime scene match Boone and his friend, Paris Geil. Also, a long dead, medical insurance salesman from Portland named Eugene Kard, who had a sideline in prostitution, gun running, extortion, and murder. The county detectives have been scratching their heads. It's not unheard of for a fingerprint to last a decade or more. But Eugene's death certificate is for 1978."

"Anything from Boone's girlfriend?"

"No, she's in the wind."

"Thanks, Dan."

For a while now, when I had time, I'd illegally staked out Bliss Schneider's place in Wish Bay.

Her cliff-top mansion had many bedrooms and en-suite bathrooms whose floor-to-ceiling windows overlooked the wild Pacific. A slate terrace at the back had a barbecue area and swimming pool.

A couple of times, I took my lunch at the edge of a forest overlooking the road that passed her property. Then I started going in the evenings, after work. Stalking, I suppose Ann would call it.

According to the National Crime Information Centre, the previous owner, Santiago Haverford-Grainger, was a seventy-three year old Cape man who went missing a few weeks before Schneider moved in.

Bliss got home, generally, at about nine or ten, on her own. Most nights, she enjoyed a glass of red wine on the terrace.

One night, Dame Teddy came by. Karl Rieper turned up in a catering van and unloaded at least a hundred, stainless steel, beer kegs. My instinct was they weren't full of beer.

I heard a twig snap in the trees behind me. A gaunt, long-haired man emerged. He wore a creased, Hawaiian shirt and smelled of sweat. There were scratches across his face and a black eye.

"Good evening, Deputy. My name is Santiago Haverford-Grainger," he said, bowing slightly.

"Aren't you supposed to be missing?"

"Don't believe everything you read, my dear."

"What are you doing here?"

"You first."

I tapped my tin star. Santiago took out a handkerchief and unwrapped a slice of fruitcake.

"This doesn't look like an official stakeout. I've seen you out here a few times, having a gander."

He broke off a piece of his cake.

"You want some?"

I shook my head. He took a bite and chewed, staring down at the house.

"Wessendorf and his coven first performed their ceremonies over there."

"I thought that was in the old Wessendorf house?"

"No, that was when he traveled in spirit. This was later when he opened an actual door. The rocks here have deep cracks."

He wrapped up his piece of cake.

"I knew your father. Before he went out there," Santiago said, gesturing towards Wish Bay.

"Out where?"

"Where people go when they go missing. The islands."

"Is he there now?"

"Don't know. I can, however, show you how to get across the Hiddensee to find out. It involves breaking and entering into my old house."

I thought for a moment. Bliss wouldn't be home until nine. We had twenty minutes.

"Come on," I said.

We slid down a grassy bank and jogged across the road. I followed Santiago around the side of the house to the slate terrace. He took a key from his pocket and opened a glass door into a pink studio room, which had an exercise bike and treadmill overlooking the ocean.

I followed him up a cool, tiled corridor. Santiago opened a door and we went into a dark basement.

He switched a flashlight on. Hundreds of beer kegs lined the walls. Pony kegs, I thought, remembering my time tending bar. Eight gallons each. Andi and Elliott had stumbled across only a fraction of the Mark 77.

The room had a concrete floor covered with a dirty, Persian rug, which Santiago rolled up. He stuck his long fingernails into a barely visible line and pulled up a hatch. It was a square of wood, disguised by an inch of concrete on top. It revealed a dark hole. Cool, damp air blew out.

"What's down there?" I said.

"A tunnel."

"Where does it go?"

Santiago stuck his head into the hole and breathed in.

"Another world."

Santiago smiled.

"Mom was a medium. She heard the voices of the missing children. Dug a tunnel to rescue them. Dad helped her. It took decades. They died before it was finished."

I knelt down and ran my hand over black rock beneath the layer of concrete.

"The cliffs here are basalt," I said.

"Correct. Very hard, volcanic. But there are seams of soil and loose rock. This tunnel mainly winds through the easy parts."

"How long is it?" I said.

"Changes every time you go down. Some days it's longer, others shorter. It goes down below the water level."

He scratched his ear.

"I finally finished it when Coffi's hired thugs came knocking."

"Did they know about the tunnel?"

"I don't know. I don't think so. But they know this place is important."

"Why didn't you use the tunnel?"

He smiled.

"The voices told my mom that to reach the Hiddensee you need a minus tide. You heard of those?"

"Yeah, my sister and I went clamming a couple of times when we were kids. An extra low tide below the normal level."

He snapped his fingers.

"Right, during a full or new moon. In two night's time, Walpurgisnacht, as the primitive folks of Cape Misfortune call it, there will be a minus tide. The submerged forest will be exposed. And the path leading to the Hiddensee. That's when I'm crossing over."

"Why, what's over there?'

"Heard a rumor you can live forever. All you need is a borrow-pence to pay the Ferryman."

He held out an ancient-looking, silver coin. Both sides were worn smooth.

A door opened upstairs. Bliss walked down the tiled corridor. Another door opened.

"She's in the bathroom," Santiago said. "Come on."

We ran through the house, across the road, and up into the trees. We watched Bliss sit on the terrace with a glass of wine.

Santiago bowed again.

"Nice meeting you, Deputy."

"Are you okay for somewhere to stay?"

"No offense, but the word is being around you is a little dangerous."

He squeezed my arm, smiled apologetically and disappeared into the shadows.

Elliott phoned me in the early morning. A buddy in the Coast Guard told him Ham Rourke was missing. They found his boat drifting near Narwak rock.

"I've come out of hiding," Elliott said.

I boarded the Mud Hen an hour later. Elliot was wearing his blue, Coast Guard uniform.

"It's Walpurgisnacht," he said. "If I was the Coffi Corporation, and I wanted to burn something, I'd do it tonight. With all the fireworks and public fires, it would take a while before anyone put two and two together. By then it would be too late."

He rubbed his chin.

"The Harbor Master told me an eighty-foot yacht called the *Andiamo* docked at Valkyrie on the day of the killings. Get this – Ed Henderson owned it."

"How could Ed afford that?"

"He bought it a week before he tried to blow us up on the roof. Paid in cash. And I found something else out from an ex-army buddy. *Mark 77* carries on burning under water."

"They're going to burn the marine reserve, not just the land," I said.

"I'm going to go and hunt for the *Andiamo*."

"Stay safe."

He laughed.

"Always."

Chapter Twenty-Six
Gone

Walpurgisnacht is Cape Misfortune's big night, celebrating the start of spring.

Every year, a parade winds its way down Valkyrie Main Street. Kids dress as fairytale characters and bang pots together to scare off evil spirits. There are fewer floats each year, or maybe it just seems that way, but old customs survive. A Misfortune council member dons a furry costume to become "Krampus" - a half-goat, half-demon creature who has somehow found his way into the spring festival.

At sundown, the town gathers to watch seven burning hay wheels roll down a hill into the water. I watched two muscular firemen light the first of the giant wheels. When it caught alight, they positioned the flaming circle and shoved, hard. The wheel wove an erratic course down the hill, picking up speed as it went along. There was a roped-off path, but the chance of a flaming hoop veering into the crowd was half the fun. I remember Aggie and me running for our lives a few times.

I watched the happy faces, lit up by the blazing circle, and felt dread for whatever was coming. The wheel trundled over the cliff edge and fell into the ocean with a splash. I half-expected it to light a deadly slick of floating napalm.

I had made my mind up to illegally search Bliss Schneider's basement when Dan Ridley tapped me on the shoulder.

"Cassie."

"Yeah?"

"They found blood on the back porch of your house. DNA matches Boone. There's an arrest warrant out for you. For murder."

"That's ridiculous."

"Frederson thinks you killed Boone at your place and then faked the abduction. There's a warrant out for Elliott, too."

"But Boone's girlfriend witnessed his kidnapping."

"She washed up dead on Ukobach beach an hour ago."

"You know bad stuff is happening on the Cape, Dan. Something big is going to happen, tonight."

"You have the right to remain silent and refuse to answer questions."

The second burning wheel rolled past. I thought I saw Cath in the crowd, dressed up in a medieval European costume, laughing and clapping.

I looked out at the ocean. A fog was rolling in.

"Bliss Schneider has a huge store of military-grade incendiary gel in her cellar," I said, as we got into the patrol car. "Ed Henderson bought a boat the day before he blew the bank up. I think they may use it to burn the park and the new nature reserve."

"Why would anyone do that?"

"The pipeline. They have to turn Cape Misfortune into a desert."

"Who is they?"

"Come on. Coffi, the Wessendorfs."

"And fae - folk from across the water. Like Cath," Dan said.

I looked at him in astonishment.

"You know about that?"

Dan shrugged.

"I'm from the Cape. I just saw Cath Claybourn in the crowd. We'll need a warrant to search Schneider's place."

"No time," I said. "People are in danger."

We pulled into Bliss's driveway. Karl Rieper was carrying a pony keg towards the open back doors of a red van. My phone buzzed.

It was a text from Elliot. "Come quickly. Have seen the *Andiamo*. Docked, waiting for cargo."

Rieper walked back to the house and stood in the doorway, arms crossed.

"Something the matter, Officers?

"What's in the keg?" I said.

He laughed.

"Beer. Just picking up a few supplies for the Walpurgisnacht bash at Captain Frederson's house."

"You mind opening one up for us?" Dan asked.

"I wouldn't know how to."

"I would," I said.

A smell of rotten meat wafted out of the house. A long-dead, insurance salesman, in a biker's vest, walked out of the doorway with a keg in each arm. He put them down in front of him.

"You can't be here. This is private property."

"Mr. Eugene Kard," I said. "I've just been reading your death certificate."

Dan did something that surprised everyone. He drew his pistol and put a round in the keg by Kard's feet. Pressurized black jelly, smelling of gasoline and laundry detergent, sprayed Eugene's jeans. We all stepped back.

Once again, my mild-mannered colleague surprised everyone. A windproof, Zippo lighter sailed towards the black ooze puddling around the keg.

"I would run if I were you," Dan warned.

I was closer to the house than Dan was, so I figured my best chance was the front door. I barged between Eugene and Rieper, and ran up the corridor. The hospital security guard chased after me and grabbed my shoulder. I shrugged him off. It felt like the air around us got sucked out. A shock wave from the exploding beer keg blew us down the tiled hallway.

I got up. The heat was so intense I could feel my hair shriveling. Rieper writhed on the floor, trying desperately to pat it out, the rivulets of burning *Mark 77* gel splattered over his back.

Further up, Eugene's motionless body was on fire.

Flames advanced up the corridor. I crawled to the basement door and tumbled down the steps.

I must have blacked out. I woke up on the floor amongst scattered pony kegs. Flame and smoke belched out of the doorway at the top of the stairs.

Rieper stood over me, Taser in hand.

I tried to suck in some air. There wasn't enough oxygen.

"Taser man," I croaked.

There were charred, bloody mounds of burnt flesh over the back of his head and neck. His beard was smoking. But I had to hand it to him - he was attempting a triumphant grin.

I went unconscious again. Two Taser electrodes hit my forehead. A hard jolt of electric current woke me up. I tried to move but couldn't.

I watched a burning line of *Mark 77* trickle down the basement steps and spill onto the laminate floor. It reached Rieper's left shoe, which burst into flame. He waved his foot around desperately. His trigger finger must have relaxed because suddenly I could move.

I crawled over to the Persian rug. Liquid oozed from a crimped crease in a dented keg beside it, leaving a black puddle.

I yanked the carpet aside and pulled the disguised hatch up. Cool, life-giving air blew out.

The leaking keg exploded. The shock wave knocked me down the hole. As the hatch blew shut, I saw a rolling sea of fire engulf Karl 'Grim' Rieper.

Part II: The Disappearance of Cassandra Dollar

Chapter One
The Ferryman

I bounced down a flight of rocky steps. Painful insults flowered over my body until I rolled over an uneven rock floor. I lay in the darkness, too exhausted to move, but enjoying the oxygen and the cool, damp air. There was no light. I could smell burnt skin - mine, I realized. My body was numb for a second; then it lit up with pain.

I opened a pouch in my gear belt and took out a small, LED flashlight. The glow revealed a chamber of dark, undressed basalt. A silk hatbox sat in the corner, covered in dust. I pulled the top off. There was no hat. A handful of faceless borrow pence lay on the bottom. I took one.

I found an entrance to a descending tunnel and went down, hunched over, so I didn't keep hitting my head. I lost track of time. Eventually, the tunnel floor became wet, and water dripped from the ceiling.

A door blocked the tunnel. It looked like the doors in the psychiatric unit – plywood, white, with a small viewing window in the top half. Wire mesh reinforced the glass.

A skull stared back at me. Its burned body was submerged up to the neck in dark water. A few scraps of charred skin and tissue clung to the bones. It had one eye left, traumatized and fearful. The shape of the face looked familiar. Then I realized. It was my face, reflected. I started back. My heel caught on a ledge in the stone floor, and I fell backward.

When I got up, the little viewing window was just a dark square. My reflected face was dirty and scratched, but not burned. I tried the door handle. Locked. I kicked the door a few times - making a dent in the wood, then a crease, then a break. The door swung open.

I walked out into a forest of dark, and dripping, Myrtlewood trees whose roots grew in cracks between the rocks. Dripping seaweed and lichen hung from the lifeless branches. The wind made a strange melody.

Soon the trees became so crowded that no moonlight got through. I squeezed blindly between the wet trunks.

Then I walked out onto a dark, rocky shore. A bright, bloated moon filled the western sky. Thousands of shallow rock pools shone like a galaxy.

I turned to see the cliffs above Wish Bay. They were on fire. I hoped Dan was alive.

I followed a meandering ribbon of bare rock between thick seaweed and crustacea. I saw Needlepoint. For the first time in my life, there was no ocean around it.

The first full moon of spring, Santiago had said. This was the minus tide, but lower than I had ever seen it.

Forgotten objects lay on the seabed – plastic bottles, trawling nets, and broken crockery. A glass beer mug had 'Ein Souvenir aus Kap Schicksal' written on it.

The path led to a vintage car with a long engine bonnet. The vehicle was so furred with seaweed, it looked like a beached sea creature. The passenger door swung open. There was a key in the ignition. I got into the cabin and turned it. The engine made a choking sound. Everything around the car seemed to flicker and go dark. I felt faint. Then moonlight lit up webbed cracks in the windshield. The world felt so ruptured and broken that no truth was possible. I fell out of the car into a tide pool. Cold water soaked into my uniform.

I continued up the little trail of bare rock. I heard the ocean. I passed under an arch that looked like the tusks of a giant animal. Ahead of me, moonlight lit a rolling line of surf.

A sleek, silver-colored yacht was anchored near the shore. I counted four decks, judging from the dark lines of smoked windows. Not quite Russian oligarch, but ostentatious for this stretch of the Pacific North West.

I waded into the surf and swam. The water felt thick as treacle, and warm. I caught a strong current, like an astral current, that swept me straight towards the boat.

Someone stood on the prow of the main deck, smoking a cigarette. There was something familiar about the defiant way he held himself.

Then I realized it was Ed Henderson, large as life, or death, I suppose. He wore a yellow jumpsuit rolled to his waist, topped with a grimy wife-beater. He twirled his hand around to indicate I should go back to where I came from.

The name *Andiamo* was written on the boat's hull.

I caught hold of a side-ladder and climbed.

When I got up to the deck, Ed had a look of puzzled dislike on his face.

"I need a lift to where my sister, Agata, went," I said.

He smiled, faintly.

"Believe me, you don't want to go there."

"You're the ferryman, right? You have to take me."

"How d'you get here, anyway? You been geschanked?"

I took out a coin and flipped it in the air. Ed caught it, then grimaced when he saw the smooth sides.

"Borrow pence. You are full of unpleasant surprises," he said, scratching his chin. "What a double disappointment. First, my cargo of *Mark 77* doesn't turn up and, now, you're on my boat ordering me around."

I followed him into a sleek cockpit that had a chrome steering wheel surrounded by control panels full of GPS, radios, radars and compasses. A computer screen displayed a map of Wish Bay.

Ed spat on the floor and pushed the throttle forward.

"Hell, let's have a party. You want a drink? There's a mini-fridge."

"No, thanks."

"Oh, that's right, you don't."

Ed was trying hard, but he had lost some of his usual swagger, I thought.

"You responsible for the non-arrival of my pony kegs?"

I didn't answer. Rain spattered on the wheelhouse's smoked window. A stream of hot air blew out of a wall panel. Steam came off my wet clothes.

"You made a big mistake coming here," Ed said. "Alive people don't cross over, not voluntarily."

"Wessendorf did. I think you did, too."

He tutted, smiling shyly.

"I was dead. There wasn't much left of my body after my martyrdom. My mortal remains were reconstituted. Took the powers-that-be a lot of effort."

We skirted the coast. It was different from the one I knew. The cliffs grew higher, until they stretched up forever, pock-marked with caves and covered in carved symbols. Now and then, shadowy shapes moved inside.

A bank of dark cloud blotted out the moon. The ocean became as black as coffee. The waves started to bulge with malignant shapes.

"This how they repaid you for murdering all those innocent people, Edwyn? Being a boat boy? I read your rap sheet. This has to be the first time you've managed to hold down a real job."

Ed laughed and wagged his finger.

"Everyone's got to earn a livin', darlin', even in the Next Life. Anyway, I kind of like this boat. I picked it out. It has a jacuzzi, pool and 3D cinema."

I looked out of the wheelhouse window. The night sky had cleared. The giant moon was now crimson. The crests of the waves looked like they were tipped with blood.

Ed studied a few navigation instruments.

"Mind if the boat boy takes a smoke break, Deputy?"

He opened a storage locker beneath the control panel and pulled out a thick, knee-length fur coat. It made him look like a frontier trapper.

"Got one for me?"

He pulled out a blue parka coat, with a crusty blood stain on the fur hood.

"It belonged to my wife," he said.

Outside, the fog smelled of charred flesh. The air was chilly. I shivered.

"It's going to get much colder where you're going."

I leaned over the side. A line of purple lights along the bottom of the lower deck shone dully onto bulging shapes in the dark water.

Ed offered me a cigarette. I shook my head. He lit one and inhaled deeply.

"We're betwixt and between here, Cassie dear. Not one place or another."

He took out the coin I gave him.

"That was clever, finding a way to get over."

The boat headed into a bank of thick crimson fog.

"Ghost fog. Kind that burns the soul, if you still have one," Ed said.

As he spoke, the giant silhouette of an old ocean liner loomed above us. Two chimney stacks bellowed glowing smoke.

"What is this?"

"A ferry."

"To where?"

"Where every mortal being goes in the end - no matter how humble or how proud. The Isle of the Dead."

The liner's hull was alive with black barnacles and crustacea who slithered in the crimson moonlight. There were figures on the decks. Motionless. All of them stared out at sea. The vessel disappeared into a bank of deeper fog.

Ed flicked his cigarette into the water.

"You're not, you know," he said.

"What?"

"Superior to me. I wasn't raised on some kiss ass, toy farm. Or in a nowhere Sheriff's Office. I sacrificed everything I had. And you know what? I'm immortal now. I'll be around until the universe dies of heat death, and beyond. You? You're just a big mouth. I don't wonder the powers-that-be are keen to shut your gob, just like they did with dear old pa."

A massive force hit the side of the boat. We were both thrown onto the deck.

"It knows you're alive. It can smell you."

"Who can?"

Something smacked into the boat's side again, sending us sliding across the deck.

"You always ruin everything," Ed said. "I'm not going to spend eternity in pieces in a sea monster's gut. Not for you, not for Krampus himself."

He jumped up.

"Time for a little chemical warfare."

A mound of glutinous, black water reared up beside the boat. Two luminous eyes appeared, dripping in gloop.

Ed opened a storage hatch in the deck, pulled out a tub of paint and pried the lid off.

"Gives these critters a serious case of indigestion. Storm Maidens, they're called. I prefer my name for them – Crocosaurus."

He swung the tub underarm a few times before letting go. The container sailed into the dark mouth, leaving a stripe of white paint along the creature's tongue.

The animal roared. The snout sank into the black water.

Ed danced a little jig.

"Now that's how you deal with a crocosaurus."

A massive jaw clamped down on the other side of the deck. The floor tilted so hard we slid helplessly towards the mouth. Ed caught on to a metal spar. I grabbed hold of his leg. The deck went vertical.

"An unexpected stroke of good fortune," Ed said. "As I'm not obliged to play ferryman to the victim of a man-eating crocosaurus."

He stamped on my head a couple of times.

Then the boat shook so hard we were both in the air again, falling towards the giant maw. I caught hold of a metal, passenger rail a few feet above the mouth. Ed grabbed my waist. The creature's hot breath covered us in beads of moisture.

The railing bent and we dipped closer to the mouth. The animal jumped upwards, biting off Ed's body above the hip.

His eyes rolled back into his head, and his arms let go. I grabbed a handful of his gold bullet chain.

His eyes righted themselves. He studied his missing legs and dangling intestines.

"Bitch," he said.

I wasn't sure if he meant the animal or me. The jaws opened up again.

Ed grabbed onto my hand with a painfully, tight grip. Then he bounced up and down, trying to dislodge me from the railing.

"You're coming with me, Cass."

I got my feet onto his shoulder and pushed down. With a scream of rage, the immortal remains of Edwyn Henderson fell into the immense darkness of the creature's belly. The mouth snapped shut. The snout sank into the dark water. The boat righted itself.

When my body stopped rolling, I lay on my back for a long while, watching flakes of snow fall from the clouds, crimson in the moonlight. Then I got up and staggered into the wheelhouse. The little space was warm – a cozy pocket of life.

"You can do this, champ," I said, to myself.

The computer display showed a square of blue ocean, which broke up and pixelated every few seconds. The diesel tank was two-thirds full according to the fuel gauge. A message at the bottom of the screen said the boat was on autopilot, cruising north-northwest. What that meant out here, I had no idea. If this was America, the *Andiamo* would be sailing to Alaska.

I picked up the radio by the wheel and tried the emergency channel.

"Mayday, Mayday, Mayday. This is the *Andiamo*. I am lost at sea."

My pleas were met with buzzing static.

A piece of yellowing paper was taped to the side of the control panel. It was a map, hand-drawn in brown ink, with the title 'Hiddensee.' Two large islands were marked 'Summerland' and 'Winterland.' A third landmass, smaller and further north, was called 'Insel der Toten.'

"Island of the Dead," I said.

Someone had ringed it with a sharpie and written: 'Avoid.'

I opened the mini-fridge. A six-pack of low-calorie beer stood beside a blood bag marked 'Rh 0 Positive.' The boat shuddered. A glass vial rolled out from the back of the fridge. Glowing, yellow-orange liquid inside swirled around like slow fire. I pulled out a plastic stopper and sniffed. It smelled sweet, like rose water with a hint of nail varnish. I dipped a finger in it. The tip became faintly luminous. I tried a sip and wished I hadn't. It felt like a red-hot skewer through my tongue. For a second everything in the wheelhouse seemed to shimmer and soften.

I checked out the locker under the instrument panel. A long sports bag contained a hunting rifle, a half-empty bottle of bourbon, a carton of cigarettes, a clasp knife, two candy bars, a compass and a cellophane-wrapped brick of cocaine. Beside the bag, I found a pair of waders, snow boots, a fur hat with flaps and some woolen mittens. I put them all on.

Then I emptied the liquor bottle over the side and packed it with snow.

I sat on the wheelhouse floor and pulled the blood-stained hood of my coat up.

I dreamt Aggie and I helped with the harvest, while Grandma watched from a chair. The Dollar sisters were hip-high in a flooded, cranberry bog pushing beating machines that knocked the berries off their vines. The red fruit floated on the surface, ready to be sucked up by a waiting truck.

It was a moment in time that felt immortal. I thought I would always be here, doing this.

We were identical twins, but her features were more delicate. I was gloomier than Aggie, winter to her summer, my mother once said. Aggie was more driven. Mom always said she would change the world.

The water in the bogs got cold. Colder than the ocean water around Misfortune in the dead of winter. Cold enough to take a life.

When I woke, water sloshed over the wheelhouse floor.

Chapter Two
Glass

The cabin was flooding fast. The bourbon bottle floated past me towards the open cabin door.

The *Andiamo's* bent nose was buried in a mountainous iceberg, surrounded by an expanse of bobbing pack ice.

I dived into the storage locker and grabbed Ed's bag.

The ship's nose broke free with a rending screech. The boat started to list on one side.

I ran up to a bedroom on the next deck, and opened the window. It was a long drop. I threw the bag over and jumped after it, hitting an ice slab and rolling across the surface.

The silver yacht turned entirely on its side, sending out waves that rippled through the floating ice pack, nearly knocking me off my new perch. Rows of dark windows disappeared under the water. Then Ed's yacht was gone.

I looked around me. I was on one of countless pieces of ice that stretched as far as I could see. I took out the compass. In the absence of a better plan, I followed Ed's course.

I spent the morning jumping between giant ice cubes jostling in a turquoise sea. There were big gaps of sea between the oval slabs but, after half a dozen successful leaps, my morale improved.

Once I hit a piece of thin ice whose opaque surface showed the water beneath. A pair of eyes stared up.

Nothing grew out here. Nothing to eat or burn. The oval slabs simply rubbed up together in an endless, soulless dance. By midday, I was shaking, with cold, or exhaustion, I couldn't tell.

In the early afternoon, the gaps between the ice started to close. The leaps got shorter. Soon I was walking on a continual sheet. I saw dark rocks peeping out of the ice.

A low-pitched, engine noise filled the air. I checked the sky through Ed's rifle sights. A silver balloon sailed across the northern horizon. A wooden boat hung beneath, with a carved figurehead at the prow - a man in a stovepipe hat.

I flattened myself and waited for the airship to cross the sky.

I kept walking. Mountains appeared on the horizon, gleaming in the afternoon sun. I saw another shadow in the sky. A bird of prey wheeled high above me, a falcon.

The wind blew hard. The snow started to drift. I concentrated on putting one foot in front of the other. I reached the foothills as the sun was setting.

A shelf of hard snow sloped against a ridge of rock. I cut blocks out of the side with Ed's knife and climbed in, stacking them up behind me. I ate a candy bar in the darkness and washed it down with a slug of meltwater from the bourbon bottle, giving myself a pep talk about not dying of hypothermia in my sleep. I dozed fitfully.

The sky got light. I crawled out, feeling woozy and having difficulty collecting my thoughts. I kept moving, finding a mountain trail that snaked between the rocks. Clouds rolled in and unburdened their cargoes of snow.

It was steep and harder going now. Gusts of bitter wind kept trying to knock me over.

The snow fell so thickly it covered the trail. My head felt numb. It was hard to remember where I was, or what I was doing out here. I could see no way through the rocks.

Then I saw a little furry animal, no bigger than a rat, in the corner of my eye. I followed it into a steep valley protected from the wind.

I leaned against a rock. A section of snow slid off. The surface reflected late-afternoon light. I ran a finger over it. It wasn't stone nor ice.

"Glass," I said.

I looked up and saw, far above me, a dark hole in the side of the strange rock.

I once spent an afternoon climbing a fake rock wall in a shopping mall. I liked it. The instructor advised never to climb without the right equipment. Today, there were no ropes to help me up - or hold me if I fell.

I climbed anyway, using hand and foot-holds I found in the glass rocks. Higher up, the wind gusted harder. Each time I squeezed against the rock face and waited for it to pass.

Then I crawled into the mountain's dark mouth. An ice ax lay by the entrance, the metal head orange with rust. The chamber was a dome of glass. It held the sunlight and felt smooth and warm to the touch.

There was a sunken basin in the middle of the room, the bottom covered in animal skins. An orb of glass at one end gave off heat. A hole in the ceiling above it seemed to serve as a chimney, though there was no smoke.

How nice to have a reprieve from death, I thought, as I collapsed onto the skins.

When I woke, the cave walls were suffused with a rich, orange-red light. The sun was setting in the valley.

There was a cooking pot on a tripod above the globe. Was it there before? The pot was filled with what looked like dried vegetables. I melted snow and boiled them. The stew tasted good.

I was woken later by a whistling wind outside. The cave wall was the color of moonlight. The wind started to moan a broken melody. Snowflakes gusted into the cave, swirling thickly in the air until an outline formed. A dark-haired woman, wearing animal skins.

"Who are you?" I asked.

She looked down at me and thought for a moment.

"The echo of a land that grieves."

"I need help."

"When my people needed help, it did not come. Nor mercy."

Her eyes weren't human. They glittered like a silver sea.

"I'm looking for my sister."

"All mine are dead."

"Sorry to hear that."

"There is an ugly place across these mountains. Keep to the direction you are going. You may find her there, if she lives."

She looked around the cave.

"Only the lost come here now. The eyes of the Imperia are everywhere, but this place is forgotten, hidden. Unseen by the enemy."

She turned and walked to the cave mouth.

Her body disintegrated into a flurry of snow before she got there.

I slept until the cave walls glittered with morning light.

I checked the compass and continued my course.

In the afternoon, the gusts of snow were so strong I could hardly see the path. But, again, the little animal appeared out of nowhere. I found another valley, and another cave high in the glass rocks.

I cooked, then lay on soft skins while the walls glowed in the sunset.

That night, I dreamt the mountain's memories. A man in a stove-pipe hat wanted to be a god. He offered only violence and desire. Steam trains and airboats crossed the land.

I dreamt of my father. His head was shaved. He had someone else's eyes. A palace had a monstrous chimney that belched black smoke, and every curl of fog was the epilogue to a sad tale. I dreamt of a Harley Lowrider sulking in a Valkyrie garage, looking for its owner.

I hiked five more days in the mountains. At night, I slept in caves bathed in light and loss.

Every morning, the food pot looked as if nothing had been taken.

Then the land flattened out and rain fell.

I came to the edge of a dark forest.

Chapter Three
A Story, A Story

As I walked, the trees became stooped and gnarled. The forest canopy closed above me. Only a few spots of dappled light fell on the path.

A cobbled road led to a square of burned-out cottages. There was a well in the center with a little, broken roof. A rank smell came out of it.

I followed a path back into the forest. The trees here stooped as if under the burden of some unsupportable weight, their trunks twisted in the effort to stay upright.

The trail dwindled into nothing. I heard the voices of children singing and followed the sound to a fire-blackened clearing. A single, ancient oak survived untouched amongst a field of charred stumps.

A body lay beneath the old tree. Three creatures hovered around it, wings whirring. They were small, like children, their skin pink and waxy; their hair long and yellow.

They threw a heavy ball between each other, singing, "I saw a little mouse, In das Krankenhaus, in das Krankenhaus,"

Something about the shape of the ball frightened me.

"It had such little feet. It scuttled, scratched and squeaked."

I knelt down and stared through the rifle sights. They were playing catch with Charlie Playfair's head. I cried out. His body lay under the oak tree, still dressed in the hospital gown he died in.

The creatures stopped singing and turned.

They flew towards me in a blur. One stuck a fingernail in the top of my hand. I cried out and dropped my rifle. Little hands grabbed my hair and dragged me over scorched earth to the exposed roots of the old oak.

One of them kicked Charlie's backside with her foot.

"His soul went walkies. So, we drank his blood."

"And everything else," said another.

"He was a good person," I said.

"You talk like a bad bean," one said.

"Bad bean, bad bean!" they chanted, clapping their hands and baring rows of sharp, blood-stained teeth.

A root from the ancient oak tree twined around my gear belt. I pushed it away.

"Let me pass," I said. "I won't be any trouble."

"Tell us a story or I won't put flowers on your grave," one said.

"Yes," the other two said. "A story, a story."

"I'm a police officer," I said. "You know what that is?"

"Someone who tells other people what to do," one said.

"Oh no, no, no," another said. "We hate a bossyboots."

My rifle lay across the clearing. I had Ed's knife on my belt.

"There was a wicked queen," I said. "Who ruled, without love or kindness, so the land was laid waste. No courtiers were brave enough to stand up to her. So they lied. When there was drought, they pretended it rained. When there was famine, they claimed there was plenty. The newspapers said it was a golden age."

"Was she pretty?"

"Who?"

"The queen, silly."

"No one knew. They never saw her. The land became a desert. Anyone who complained, disappeared."

"Quite right."

I got ready to move.

"So many disappeared, there was no one to plow the fields, scatter the seeds or harvest the crops. There was no kingdom left to rule. So, the queen disappeared along with everyone else."

"Is that it?" one said.

"Where did all the disappeared people go?" another asked.

I stood up.

"Some were dead. Some made perilous journeys to far-off lands. But all of the disappeared people knew where they were - even if nobody else did. That's why no one ever really disappears."

I reached under my coat and took out Ed's hunting knife.

"I'm going," I said.

I walked across the burned-out clearing towards my rifle. They let me get to the edge, then little hands grabbed my hair and pulled me high above the trees.

I saw a cluster of massive buildings beyond the forest edge. A metal pipeline stretched off into the distant mountains.

"Let her down, girls," a familiar voice from below me said.

Cath Claybourn waved up at me. A gold braid hung from her shoulder above the row of new medals.

They dropped me at her feet. Cath cradled a long, single-barreled rifle in her arms.

"How the tables have turned," she said. "Deputy Dipsomaniac, come all the way out to the Next Life."

She held up a silver dart with a feather quill and slid it into the breach of her gun.

"You can run if you like, sweetie."

And so I did. There was a sharp pain in the back of my neck. Then darkness.

Chapter 4
The Krankenhaus

You have been here before. A monstrous, dark, cathedral-sized building framed against a leaden sky. Where endless corridors echo to the involuntary cries of human agony. Where the crowded wards are full of busy, incurable patients. A psychiatric hospital of the imagination.

The brass plaque on the door said 'Kerdus Krankenhaus: A Facility for the Treatment of Hysterical Women'.

The ward had long rows of beds with patients in various stages of malnutrition. The male orderly, sitting beside the door, had a long, handlebar mustache and wore a buttoned-up, white tunic. He read a newspaper in the light of an electric lamp, now and then flicking cigarette ash into a heaped ashtray.

The nurse who wheeled me inside had 'KK' engraved on her belt buckle. The backs of her hands were covered in thick fur. A silver revolver hung from a holster on her belt.

"My name is Nurse Eva. You go to sleep, young lady. Maybe you'll have some nice dreams."

A needle punctured my neck.

The orderly heaved me onto a bed. I felt numb, like I was lying on a frozen field somewhere.

I dreamt of the Wish Bay cliffs awash with burning *Mark 77*, while someone I loved rode through the fog.

I woke to watch the dawn in the ward's high, skylight windows. The sleeping orderly's head had lolled forwards. His long mustache dangled over his belly.

I tried to move. My arms were bound across my chest. When I looked up, the orderly stood beside me.

"Stop wriggling so bloody much, or I will give you a slap. Or worse," he said.

"I need the bathroom."

"You get a toilet privilege later like everyone else. This isn't a hotel."

"I'm a United States police officer. Take these restraints off me."

The back of his hand hit my cheek, hard.

"Shouldn't speak, 'less you're spoken to."

A tall, stooped man with baggy pouches under his eyes came into the ward with a mop and bucket. He had a waist-length, white beard tucked into a broad belt. His dark eyes opened in surprise when he saw me.

Later, the orderly with the handlebar mustache strapped me into a wicker wheelchair.

Eva pushed me outside. Snow fell from a dirty sky.

"Where are we going?" I said.

"The vice. They are going to press you. If you haven't got any juice in you, they'll cut your body up for spare parts."

"You have no right to do this to me."

Eva stuck her face close to mine. A thick stubble of fur emerged through the skin of her flushed cheeks.

"Sass me again, and I'll sew up that gob of yours, so you have to take your meals through a nose tube."

Her breath smelt of bacon. A string of brown saliva hung between two rows of sharp teeth. The hair went back into her face.

She consulted her fob watch and wheeled me towards an ancient stone building with a domed roof.

We went into a rectangular waiting area. An orderly sat behind a desk reading a newspaper. His head, including his face, was covered in thick red fur. A moist nose and mournful eyes looked out at us.

"Patient Dollar 48194. Exploratory extraction," Nurse Eva said.

The man typed something on the keyboard of a bulky, old computer.

"You can go straight through," he said.

Eva wheeled me into a domed chamber. A dentist-style chair stood in the middle surrounded by banks of steel machines.

A neat, elderly man with slicked-back, white hair and prominent false teeth smiled at us. He wore a surgical tunic with a pen in his breast pocket.

"Good morning, Nurse Eva."

"Good morning, Doctor Deacon-Weiss."

He saw me looking at the machinery.

"Fascinating, aren't they? Courtesy of Julius Wessendorf, may he live forever."

Nurse Eva injected something in my neck. The red-haired orderly heaved me into the chair. The doctor stuck metal electrodes over my body, which he hung wires onto.

"I see, from your notes, that you have a twin sister here. Young Agata was an excellent manna cow. A wonderful donator. You better hope it runs in the family. We don't like time-wasters at the Krankenhaus donation center."

"Will this kill me?" I asked.

"Heavens, no. We are going to extract manna, or essence, from you. We like to keep our donors alive as long as we can."

His voice seemed far away.

The ceiling was covered in ancient carvings of women being operated on by dog-headed priests.

Nothing happened for a few seconds. The light flickered. Then my heart raced so fast, I thought it would burst. I couldn't breathe. The room swam. It felt like I was sweating all over my body. I felt trickles of luminous liquid leave me to run down the wires.

The doctor clapped his hands.

"Yes, yes. Manna."

The room went dark, and the air became icy.

"Please stop doing this," I said.

"I told you," Eva said, from somewhere far off. "A real smart-mouth."

I felt as if I was evaporating, disappearing. Then I passed out.

I woke on the ward.

An orderly dumped a small, red-headed teenager on the bed beside mine.

She looked over at me. Her eyes were bloodshot.

"Not seen you before," she whispered.

"Just got here. You from Cape Misfortune?"

"Yeah."

"What's your name?"

"Josie."

"I'm Cassie. I'm a county deputy. I remember you. Josie Oberhausen. They found your clothes on Ukobach beach."

"A fat guy beat me up and took them off me."

She coughed. It didn't sound good.

"You know a little girl called Sasha Hamrick?" I asked. "She was taken a few days ago."

"Not everyone comes to the donation facility. She's not old enough to give manna. She could be taken to the Winter Garden to be an indentured slave."

"Where's that?"

"A bad place, out to sea. The capital of this hell we're in."

The orderly with the long mustache stretched his arms.

"What about a patient called Agata Dollar?"

"Sorry. My memory sucks. One of the things that goes first."

"I need to find her."

"I ran once. They hunt you down. A lot of the staff here are half wolf. They can smell you."

"Keep those traps shut. Wolves got good ears as well as noses."

He bared his teeth and let out a little snarl.

In the afternoon, we exercised in a snowy courtyard.

In the evening, we went to a room with long wooden benches where soup was ladled into tin bowls. Orderlies and nurses stood around the table watching us.

I sat beside Josie.

"What do they do with the stuff they take from us?"

"Heard it keeps dead people alive. Most of the Krankenhaus staff are dead. Undead."

The soup was gloopy and grey, with a few peas floating in it. I looked at the haggard faces around the table. Aggie was not one of them.

"Eat up and enjoy your free meal, greedy gannets," Eva said.

That night, I dreamt I was on the cliffs by Wish Bay, standing in the ruins of Bliss's house. Charlie Playfair appeared beside me, wearing the same dark clothes and jacket he wore as the Levitator.

The grass and trees on the cliff were all burned.

"It would have been much worse if you hadn't stopped them," he said. "The whole Cape would have burned."

"How can I be here? Am I dreaming?"

He took my hand and kissed it.

"I find it hard to tell the difference nowadays. But, yes, it's good to see you."

"Patrick's parents took your body off life support," I said.

"Roy and Ellen. They had their final revenge."

The scene changed to the dark auditorium of the Venice City Arts Centre. I sat in the front row of the audience. Charlie stood on stage, in a spotlight.

"The Levitator was my way back into life after Patrick."

"What happened to you, Charlie, after your cord was cut?"

"A riptide dragged me to a far-off island where lines of people were shuffling into a dark cave. I knew from Diedrich's map it was the Isle of the Dead. I was so angry with Patrick's killers, with my killers, that I fought."

"Good for you."

"There was a mountain above the cave. It had a dead forest around it. I fought the tides for days until I got hold of a branch. I climbed down and got into the trees. I met other lost souls there. I wandered for days. One morning, I thought I heard Patrick call my name. I followed the noise to a clearing. I went up into the air. I had cheated death. I roamed over Summerland and Winterland. I saw abandoned places; cities, towns, and temples. I heard stories in strange languages. I entered the dreams of strangers and finally planned my revenge."

The scene changed to my back porch. Charlie sat in the rocking chair he had bought me.

"A powerful Imperia seer returned me to my body. They tried to make me join them."

"What did you do?"

"I escaped again. I found a geschank and cut the cord myself."

Then we were in the Krankenhaus. The patients, and the orderly at the door, were asleep. I lay strapped to the bed. The rain rattled the windows high above us. Charlie's body outline was opaque and shimmering, his voice like the arctic wind.

"Sorry to see you here, Cassie. I can't stay visible for long. It takes too much energy. I have to rest in the earth."

"What does Wessendorf want? What is this all about?"

He leaned forward. His eyes were filled with orange fire.

"Julius Wessendorf will destroy our world a piece at a time. Like with Cape Misfortune - desecrate the sacred places, poison the sea and the land. Create broken landscapes so terrible they have their own gravity of despair - where he and his goons can rule as gods."

His body started to fade. He closed his eyes and went silent for a second.

"Julius is building a new pipeline between our worlds. He wants to rule over the worlds of the living beginning with Cape Misfortune, a stepping stone to other worlds."

"Any ideas on how I can find Aggie and get out of here, Charlie?"

He smiled.

"Look for my friend, Mr. Winterbeard. The last of an old, and extraordinary, race of levitators."

The orderly opened his eyes. Charlie winked at me. Then he was gone.

In the morning, before dawn, I had a less welcome visitor. A face peered through the high window. A hand punched the glass. Shards of glass fell over me.

Dame Teddy Champion swooped down, beating long, blistered wings. Her face so badly scorched that one of her cheeks was burned open. A crusty, luminous scab of dried mucous had collected beneath a broken nose.

An alarm went off. The orderly took out a pistol and shouted for help.

Teddy unstrapped my wrists, grabbed my head in the crook of her elbow and carried me upwards through the window.

The orderly fired. Teddy grunted but kept moving.

Then we were in cold air above the Krankenhaus roof. We flew across snow-swallowed fields to a stone circle in the mountains. The carved-out ledge was on a jutting rock so high as to be inaccessible to the wingless.

Teddy dumped me in front of a tall throne. She sat and wagged her finger.

"Why do you think I always let you live, despite your constant disobedience?"

"I don't know."

"Because I loved you. I gave you every chance. Poor Bliss and I were drinking wine on the terrace when the fire came. My dear sweet girl was burned alive, because of you. I can't imagine how anyone as dreary as you, Cassandra Dollar, could be so ungrateful and cruel."

"I was doing my job."

She stood up.

"Blowing up beautiful women in oceanfront properties is not your job!"

She started to weep.

"My poor sweet darling Karl as well. He was a frightful booby but such a muscular, dearly beloved servant."

She pointed at me.

"I wanted to love you, Cassie, but you're such little people, tiny, tiny, tiny. You don't see the bigger picture. I did. I wasn't always a big cheese. I made a choice. Dear Julius Wessendorf, terrible man that he is, has big plans. Not just for your world, or mine, but for infinite worlds. Neverending conquest, like the Roman Empire, but with immortal dead people. Bellum Romanum aeternum, darling."

She made a kind of snuffling sound and patted me on the head.

"I've been sent home to be punished."

"I couldn't let them burn the Cape."

Teddy sat on the throne and waved her hand dismissively.

"I never really fit in your world. I went to one of those dreary, English boarding schools. I loved the cruelty but hated being there, darling. Everything was so conventional. I hate that. Hate humans, actually."

"Teddy, let me go."

"They will take away my burn allowance. Do you know what that means?"

"No."

"Death, real death."

"I'm sorry."

She pushed her broken nose back into place.

"I was a smashing psychiatrist. I loved my patients. I loved you."

"What happened to Sasha Hamrick?"

Teddy raised an eyebrow.

"Superb, new parents. A simply wonderful house bursting with servants and nannies."

"Where?"

Teddy shook her head.

"Don't be a bore and keep asking. It's so dreary."

"Teddy, please."

"She's dead!" she shouted, putting her hands around my neck and pushing me towards the circle's edge.

My bare feet slid on the icy rock.

"I love you."

She stopped for a second. Her moist eyes studied me. Then she pushed again.

"A cheap tactic. The only thing you've ever really loved is finding your loser family."

I tried to stop her, but she was too strong.

"Please."

"Boring, darling, boring," she said, and pushed me over the edge.

I fell into the cold air, full of despair, afraid of death, angry at Teddy, but angrier at my complete failure.

A pair of hands caught me.

"You're a stick in the spokes of everyone's wheel, Cassie," Cath Claybourne said.

We flew up to the stone circle. Teddy was sitting on the rock throne, weeping. Cath took a rifle off her shoulder and broke it open on her knee.

"Sorry, Teddy. Cassie's manna is too valuable to the Imperia. How do you want to play this?"

"The not-so-beautiful Deputy Cath," Teddy said. "We had such larks. Why does everyone I love betray me?"

Cath pushed a dart into the breach. Teddy sighed.

"So, save that horrible human and betray your own kind, eh? How ghastly."

Cath aimed and shot. Teddy put a hand to her neck.

"I was like a mum to you," she said. "I wish I hadn't bothered, darling."

She slumped forward.

Cath had tears in her eyes.

Doctor Denton-Weiss pressed me that morning. Afterward, I lay in the ward watching the janitor with the pouchy eyes and waist-length beard mop the floor. After half an hour cleaning the rest of the ward, he pushed my bed to one side, wiping underneath.

"My name is Mr. Cecil Winterbeard. The Levitator has visited my dreams."

"Cassandra Dollar," I said. "I knew Charlie when he was alive."

"Your sister talked about you. And your farm, in America, the otherworld – the place called Cape Misfortune."

"Is Agata alive?"

"She is near death. Too many donations."

"Can you get us out of the Krankenhaus?"

He stopped mopping.

"The language of my people is forgotten. Wessendorf murdered our old and young. Took essence from the women. Turned us into slaves. That's how the

Imperia works. An offense against creation, because every being is a precious thing - a universe unto itself."

"I agree. When can we go?"

He pushed my bed back.

"I need burn - distilled manna. It's strictly rationed and jealously guarded."

"I came here wearing a coat. It had a glass tube in an inside pocket. They may not have found it."

I described the parka to him. He squeezed his mop into a bucket.

"Very well. Wait for the next fog. Be ready."

Chapter Five
Canis

At midnight, I woke from a drugged sleep, stretched, and realized my arms were free. The straps were unbuckled. The orderly with the handlebar mustache was asleep.

The shade of Charlie Playfair stood by my bed.

"I'm not leaving without Aggie," I whispered.

"Come on then," the Levitator said. "And be careful. The nurses here are armed."

The Krankenhaus felt like a town with a roof, connected by a maze of dusty corridors. Charlie scouted ahead, his form flickering and weakening with each minute. We went past wards full of young women. There was a factory wing where silent, shrunken patients sat beneath massive, copper distilleries filling bottles with glowing burn.

Charlie's form flickered for a few seconds, before coming back.

"The sleeping beauty unit is next," he said.

I came to a sign that said 'High-Dependency Unit.'

Veils hung over dozens of beds. Rows of emaciated women lay motionless, covered in diodes and wires, sweating their last manna. I scanned a few faces. Then I found Agata. My sister looked smaller and younger than me, almost like a girl.

"Aggie? It's Cassie."

Her pale, drawn face was immobile. I started pulling wires off her.

"There's a wheelchair over there," Charlie said. "I'll meet you outside. Hurry."

A low fog hung over the garden. Mr. Winterbeard handed me my Venice County uniform, along with Ed's hunting rifle, knife, and coat.

"I have a friend in the processing office," he said.

A shrill alarm went off in the building. I took out the vial of slow-swirling burn. Mr. Winterbeard opened it and took a gulp. Then he hoisted Aggie over his shoulder with surprising strength.

"Come on then," he said.

The thick snow in the garden slowed us down. We crossed into a copse of tall pines by the edge of a frozen lake.

Charlie reappeared. He was as insubstantial as the fog.

"Here comes the cavalry," he said.

A Harley Lowrider fell from the sky and bounced on the ice a couple of times before sliding across the lake's freezing surface to Charlie's feet.

A ghost motorcycle emerged from the motorbike's body and stood upright.

"Good luck, everyone," Charlie said, climbing on the bike and dissolving into the air.

There was a crackling sound in the pine tree above us. Something fell through a thick canopy of branches and dropped into the snow. Elliott sat up.

"That was intense, and painful," he said.

"How did you get here?"

"It's been a weird evening."

I helped him up. He kissed me.

"Good to see you, Cassie. Sheriff's Office said you were killed in the explosion."

A shrill alarm sounded in the grounds. A bank of electric lights flooded the misty woods. It lit up a wooden boathouse on the far side of the lake.

We ran across the ice. Wolves howled in the trees. Mr. Winterbeard opened the boathouse doors to reveal a wooden rowing boat, set in the ice.

"Everyone, get in."

"Why?" Elliott said.

"It has been many years since the levitating ceremony has been performed," Mr. Winterbeard said, pulling two oars from a rack on the wall. "I'm hoping for a miracle."

The old wolfman took a long pull of swirling, orange liquid and began chanting in a lost language, gently touching the side of the boat with his fingertips. A luminous shimmer spread out from his hand across the wood.

Wolves poured out of the trees onto the frozen lake, barking and howling.

"Over there!" a voice shouted.

Mr. Winterbeard's face elongated into a snout. He went into a kind of canine ecstasy, dribbling, and whimpering. His eyes glittered like a silver sea. The boat rocked a few times before breaking free and mounting the ice. The keel of our little vessel scraped along the frozen surface.

Then we were outside.

"I take it back," Elliott said.

A pack of wolves, some still in their orderly uniforms, burst through the trees onto the frozen lake.

Our boat picked up speed, lifting a few inches in the air before falling to the surface again.

Elliott hit a wolf with the blade of an oar. The animal jumped into the boat and sunk its teeth in his arm. I wrestled to get its jaw open, while Elliott heaved it overboard.

"Cecil, we need something to happen," I said.

The ice swarmed. Wolves came in every direction.

Then Mr. Winterbeard stopped singing.

The boat lifted off, swaying erratically from side to side as we began a miraculous flight up into the cold night air. Soon, we were too high for the wolves to jump up.

The boat sailed through the trees, weaving precariously between tall pine trunks. The branches at the top of the canopy nearly knocked us off, as if trying to stop our escaping. A chorus of frustrated wolves howled as we made it in the open air.

The forest sank beneath us. Our little boat flew high above the moonlit buildings of the Krankenhaus.

"Always interesting hanging around you, Cassie," Elliot said.

Mr. Winterbeard, his eyes pools of molten silver, guided us silently over snowy gardens and outbuildings, before crossing into open country.

"Where are we going?" I asked.

"We must cross the mountains. If we're lucky, we may find help for your sister."

The frozen lakes and fields of Winterland went by below us. I lay beside Aggie, out of the wind, and cradled her in my arms. Elliott lay on the other side. His fingers touched mine. We looked up into the night sky and saw a river of stars.

I must have slept because when I sat up, the sun was in the east and we were high above the peaks of steep mountains. There were long stretches of forest in the deep valleys between them.

Mr. Winterbeard's eyes were still silver-colored.

"How are you doing, Cecil?" I asked.

"Our holy people flew for thousands of years. Although not for long distances. A journey like this takes distilled manna. Burn has destroyed our world. Once, we extended life with the holy sap for a few hours, so the dead could say their goodbyes. Now, thanks to the science of Julius Wessendorf, it can bestow eternal life."

"With essence stolen from people like Aggie," I said.

"Yes."

The boat shuddered and dropped. Elliott sat up.

"Everything okay?"

Mr. Winterbeard held out the manna bottle. It was empty.

I looked over the side. A river snaked through thick forest. There were wooden buildings dotted amongst the trees.

"Where are we?" I said.

"A mountain country once known as Canis, the Wolf Kingdom. Now it has no name. This river will take us to the sea," Mr. Winterbeard said.

The rowing boat was losing height, fast. The metal head of a spear sliced through the side, cutting the palm of my hand

Wolves ran amongst the trees.

Mr. Winterbeard slumped forward. We splashed into the fast-flowing water.

Elliott handed me an oar.

"Keep her away from the rapids," he said.

The wolves kept pace with us along the riverbank. I saw one of the animals morph into human form and shoot an arrow.

There was a wide net slung across the river. Our boat hit it and swung sideways. Then we were tangled in rope. Freezing water poured into our vessel. One side of the net was released. We swung to the riverbank.

Our captors howled as they heaved us ashore.

"My name is Cecil Aubrey Winterbeard. I am pack," Mr. Winterbeard said.

"Not my pack, you dirty old traitor," a woman's voice said.

"We are enemies of the Imperia," Mr. Winterbeard said.

"Good," another voice said. "Then you'll fetch a good price."

Our net was dragged through the snow. The wolves were human now, picking animal skins off the trees.

They stopped in the space between a circle of stone huts and cut us out of the net.

"This all of them?" a female voice asked.

"My sister isn't well," I said.

Hands pushed us down stone steps into an underground chamber full of people.

There was a smoking fire pit in the middle.

We were pushed into a kneeling position. Elliott laid Aggie on the floor.

I counted around thirty of them.

Two sat in high-backed chairs.

The woman on the throne had a thin face. A scar ran along her neck. She studied us closely.

"Thank you for allowing us into your den hall," Mr. Winterbeard said.

The man in the other chair raised a bushy eyebrow.

"You won't be grateful in a few minutes, lapdog; I can promise you that."

"They have trespassed upon our territory. Their lives are forfeit," the woman said.

"My real name is Trueluck," Mr. Winterbeard said, as he stood up. "I was born a few miles from here, by the old waterfall. My pack were amongst the first victims of the Imperia."

The wolves all watched him now.

The man with the bushy eyebrows opened a wooden chest beside him. It contained a few glass vials of glowing green liquid.

"Once the manna ran in rich veins beneath the earth. Now the land's essence is siphoned into Imperia refineries, to service people like you, Trueluck," he said.

"Soon, we will have to decide on which form to take. Wolf or man," the woman beside him said.

Mr. Winterbeard looked around the hall.

"We all exist only as a whisper of what we were. Slaves. The living working for the dead."

"Yet you took Krampus's Shilling," the woman said.

"To my shame," Mr. Winterbeard said, lowering his head.

Bushy eyebrows sighed and stood up.

"My name is Tobit."

"And I am Enlilbani," the woman said.

Mr. Winterbeard rose from his knees and sniffed noses with them.

"If we trade them, we could make enough manna to survive for another year," a voice in the crowd said.

Mr. Winterbeard pointed to Aggie, who lay in front of me.

"This girl is a changer, a powerful one, from the Otherworld."

Aggie stirred a little as he spoke. Her body briefly seemed to glow.

"In Summerland there is a place where we may heal her. So, choose between a few drops of manna or this changer – who may deal the Imperia a mortal blow."

The wolves looked at each other.

"Personally I'd prefer to take a gamble and live in hope," Tobit said. He smiled bleakly.

"Why not?" Enlilbani asked.

The wolves made a few barking sounds.

Enlilbani wrapped Aggie in a blanket. Elliott carried her to our boat.

Pale afternoon light glittered on fast-flowing water. We floated downstream, dipping the oars now and then to keep a straight course.

"The TV news said you were dead," Elliott said. "Along with Bliss and Teddy. Handsome Hank is trying to pin the whole thing on you."

"Did Dan Ridley make it?"

"He did."

"They won't try and burn the Cape now. It would be too suspicious."

"Maybe," Elliott said. "Whoever they are, they're so powerful they don't seem too worried about what people think."

"How did you get here, anyway?"

"I kept dreaming about Charlie's bike. It said it was missing him. It told me it was in Charlie's garage. When I got there, something hit the door so hard it left a bump in the metal. I opened the door, and Charlie's Harley rolled out, keys in the ignition, motor running. It took me to Wish Bay. There was a fog hanging over the ocean, like the ghost of a landscape. We went straight over the edge of the cliff. I stayed on because I knew, somehow, you weren't dead. I rode a ribbon of thick fog. Then the bike hit a tree. I fell at your feet."

"I'm glad you did," I said.

A harsh, chemical smell came from upriver, like bleach and nail varnish. A castle appeared on the river bank. It had a tall clock tower. A fiery, red circle burned where the clock should have been.

Foaming brown effluent poured out of concrete chutes into the river.

Beneath the castle walls, dozens of stooped figures loaded sections of metal pipe onto a steam-driven barge.

Farther up the riverbank, a group of soldiers in dark uniforms looked over at us. One fired a rifle. A bullet sent up a plume of water beside the boat.

The soldiers ran along the river bank. There was a ragged volley of rifle shots. A bullet hit the hull.

The fast flowing river took us back into the forest.

"That was a Stitching Factory," Mr. Winterbeard said. "Where bodies are sewn up, and limbs swapped before being stitched together and revived with burn to work in mines or build pipes for the Imperium."

"I hope you're right about Aggie being a changer," I said. "Things need to change."

Mr. Winterbeard chuckled.

"Change is manna, change is life."

Chapter Six
The Storm Maidens

The poisoned river widened into a shallow channel of brown water that flowed into the sea. The black silhouette of an airship descended through the clouds above us. A line of guns poked out of the steel gondola, like cannons on a pirate ship.

"Imperia warship," Mr. Winterbeard said. "Full of highly-trained thugs. Unfortunate."

He pointed to a stand of pine trees on the opposite shore.

"We'll land over there."

A flash of light came from the airship's metal hull as we beached our rowing boat. A rocket whistled by and exploded in nearby trees.

"What now?" Elliott said, carrying Aggie in his arms.

The old wolfman broke into a shambling run through the trees, unbuttoning his tunic. Clusters of grey fur sprouted over his body. A wolf fell forward onto four legs.

The airship loomed over the treetops. Bullets from a high-caliber machine gun splintered pine bark.

Rockets took out our abandoned boat and most of the nearby trees. Dark smoke and bright flames filled the woods, forcing us onto a snowy beach.

Mr. Winterbeard appeared beside us, buttoning up his shirt.

"The Levitator has made arrangements," he said.

He unknotted a handkerchief and held out a collection of leaves – long, waxy and red-colored.

"One each," he said. "From the last gilly-tree that grew in my land. They are rich in old manna."

"What do we do with them?" Elliott asked.

"When you are underwater, breathe in through the leaf, out through your nose. One tends to overthink these things, so don't."

"What about Aggie?" Elliott said.

"Place one between her teeth."

The sea was the color of milky coffee and littered with dark islands of frozen waste. Mr. Winterbeard bit on a leaf and splashed into a watery channel between two blocks of dirty ice.

"Follow the werewolf," Elliot said.

We ran down the beach. The warship blocked out the sun. Ropes dropped from the sky. Men in black uniforms abseiled down.

The water was shockingly cold. I closed my lips around the gillyleaf, and tried to breathe. I got a mouthful of seawater. I shut my eyes, relaxed, and tried again. This time, to my surprise, a little air came. The next time, my lungs filled with oxygen. The cold water became bearable.

We swam under icebergs of frozen sewage. Elliott held Aggie beneath him.

Black liquid hit the surface, and spread over the water until the sea-bed was dark. There was a roaring sound. Veins of orange light streaked overhead as the dark fluid burnt. Fat gobs of flame rained into the water around us. I saw Elliott's leg get hit. I was hit in the shoulder and burnt my hand brushing it off.

Soon, the ocean floor fell away and we were in the deep arctic water, navigating between rocks of icy waste. The ocean cleared of dirt and the pack ice above us turned white.

The enemy warship gave up, probably thinking the fire, or the cold, had killed us.

Despite sub-zero temperatures, green fauna grew on the seabed, shining faintly with manna.

Three dark forms swam towards us, moving fast. They closed in, resembling the huge animals Ed called Crocosauruses. They looked like oversized, grey whales from the coast back home but these animals had giant ears set back in their heads and bright, red fins. Their skin was oily, their eyes yellow and luminous beneath a glowing tusk in their forehead.

Mr. Winterbeard swam over to one of the creatures and spread his fingers against its sleek skin. They stayed in silent conference for a minute. Then he climbed onto the animal's head, holding the tusk. He gestured at us to do the same.

When we climbed up, the storm maidens blew giant bubbles out of their ears and shook their fins.

We sped through the ocean.

"Once manna nourished every plant and creature – but the holy sap's ability to perform miracles - to allow swimming between worlds - brought Wessendorf," a voice in my head said.

"My name is Cassie," I thought.

"I have many names. One is Light in Water."

The pack ice above us flew past but it never felt like I would fall off. In fact, I hardly felt any current at all. After a while, I closed my eyes. When I woke, a pale morning sun lit the dappled face of the water.

Voices told us to let go. As we drifted to the surface, the storm maidens swam out to sea.

We soon emerged in a roaring surf that broke over clean white sand.

It was a hot day. A stone path, with columns on either side, led to a doorway carved in the cliffs. Giant statues of cats with human-like bodies stood guard on each side.

"The manna still lingers in Summerland," Mr. Winterbeard said. "There is a cedar forest beyond the mountains where it always rains. A lake where it is always night, so be careful. Nothing here is what it seems."

We went into an oval amphitheater, surrounded by rows of tiered seats, all carved out of the cliff. Glass rocks in the stone ceiling captured the outside daylight, like the glass caves in Winterland.

Mr. Winterbeard unfolded a silk map. He pointed to one of many doorways leading out of the chamber.

We followed him up a square tunnel.

"How long did you work at the Krankenhaus, Mr. Winterbeard?" I said.

"So long I can barely recollect the forests of my childhood," he said.

"How could you work in that terrible place?"

"When the Imperia came, I watched my people being murdered one by one. We were given the choice of serving the Imperia or death. Some were greedy for the immortality Wessendorf promised. But most chose to die with honor. When it came to my turn, I forgot who I was.

"I'm glad you finally remembered," Elliott said.

"Before the Imperia, the dead creatures were hunted by the living and kept in check. When Wessendorf came, they killed our gods and ruled over us. Years later, a Levitator from the Otherworld reminded me who I once was."

We came out into a market square surrounded by empty stone rooms. The ground was covered in overturned tables and stalls.

"What happened here?" Elliott said.

"They refused to trade with the Imperia, I imagine. We should rest. Later we will walk in the cool of the night."

Elliott laid Aggie on the floor. Her face was expressionless. Mr. Winterbeard lay down next to her and closed his eyes.

Elliott looked over a circular wall into a stone well.

"There's a well. Can we drink this?"

"Yes," Mr. Winterbeard said. "My map says a river beneath this city flows into the sea."

I walked around the square. The stone rooms were all empty until I found a place littered with bones and beheaded cat statues. The floor was littered with bones.

"Looks like people died here," Elliott said

I followed him into a nearby empty room.

"Thanks for coming out here, I mean, from Cape Misfortune," I said.

He shrugged. There's nothing left of me, I thought; my heart has been cut out. But I kissed him.

Chapter Seven
Mr. Winterbeard's Sacrifice

The glass ceiling rocks cast a fading light over the square.

Mr. Winterbeard had found a straw hat to go with his white orderly uniform.

After trudging through a warren of tunnels, we left the cave through a door in the cliff and trekked across starlit sand dunes.

Elliott carried Aggie. After an hour of exhausting trekking, the dunes flattened out. The old wolf studied his map.

"Pyro. City of fire. We should be there soon, if we're not already."

I found a half-buried, broken bowl and picked it up. The wind blew so hard we couldn't see. It whistled around objects that didn't exist. When it died down, a stone hut had appeared in front of us.

A dark-skinned woman sat cross-legged on the floor. Her white hair was braided into cornrows. She ground wheat between a mill made of two rotating stone discs. Powdery meal spilled onto a cloth.

Mr. Winterbeard bowed slightly.

"Queen of Stars. We are the ones the Levitator told you about."

The woman grabbed a handful of meal and threw it in the air. The powder floated upwards, high into the air, before exploding in white light.

The ground beneath us rumbled so hard we fell over. Fountains of sand jetted into the air. The landscape around us bulged with new dunes.

Rooftops emerged from the sand. Stone columns punched through the earth like fists. A massive dome rose to fill the skyline. An entire city sprung up around it.

Then it was quiet. The buildings were dark. The pots and jars were empty. Everything waited.

"Where are the people who lived here?" I said.

"Sleeping. Dreaming of better times," the woman said. "These things you see are just a broken bowl you found in the wilderness. Or the writing on a wall that cannot be read."

Storm clouds gathered in the sky.

We followed the Queen of Stars along a stone avenue towards the dome. Statues of human-cat hybrids lined the way.

She opened a door into a great hall. The marble walls had carved reliefs that told stories of vanished people.

A black altar lay in the middle of the domed room. It was surrounded by a circle of chairs that looked like the ones we found in the attic of the old Wessendorf house, with metal grips at the end of each armrest.

The Queen of Stars turned to us.

"Who will stand sacrifice?"

Elliott and I looked at each other.

Mr. Winterbeard held up his hand.

"Mr. Wolf. So it be," she said.

"Wait. What does that mean?" I said.

The woman shrugged.

"Sacrifice? One in, one out," the old woman said. "One life for another - the hardest law. Someone is happy because someone is sad."

"But Aggie's not dead," Elliott said.

"Not quite," the woman said. "But, Mr. Wolf is not alive either."

"I would appreciate it if we could proceed with the ceremony," Mr. Winterbeard said, sitting on a chair at the foot of the altar.

The old woman gestured for Elliott to lay Aggie on the stone block.

"I am happy to have met you," Mr. Winterbeard said. "And wish you success in your great endeavor."

The Queen of Stars took the chair on the opposite side and closed her eyes. Darkness gathered in the hall. The old wolf and the old woman gripped the metal rods and chanted together quietly. There was a rumble of thunder outside. Mr. Winterbeard's ghost rose out of his body. It was the shade of a younger man, lean and fierce.

I had a sudden terror that I was burning to death in Bliss's house. Or psychotic in the little isolation booth in intensive care. A hysteric, not respected or believed.

I could feel Aggie's soul knitting together, growing heavier.

Mr. Winterbeard's spirit drifted upwards on an astral tide. It was wolf-shaped. The astral cord in his ankle snapped, and the old man's soul passed out of the dome.

His body slumped onto the floor.

Aggie sat up and stretched.

"You shouldn't have come for me, Cassie," Aggie said. "It was too dangerous."

Her eyes fell on Mr. Winterbeard's motionless body.

"Trueluck."

"He stood sacrifice for you," I said.

The Queen of Stars got up.

"Now leave, unless you want to be buried under the sand. The city is tired."

Aggie slid off the stone and looked at us.

The ground rumbled. The temple sank like it was in quicksand. Stone columns lining our way slid downwards. The path beneath us disappeared under the sand.

A hard wind blew in our eyes. When we opened them, Mr. Winterbeard, the Queen of Stars - and the entire city of Pyro - had gone.

Chapter Eight
Slavers

We sheltered from the sun, in the shadow of a boulder, where the hut had been. A half-buried grain mill lay in the sand.

"You're one of Venice County's finest," my twin sister said, tapping the metal star on my uniform shirt. "That was what I wanted to do."

"Maybe you still can."

She laid against the rock.

"How long is it since I went missing?"

"Nine years, give or take."

Aggie shook her head.

"Nine years of being squeezed like a lemon. Day in, day out. They gave us the tenth day off. You recovered enough to realize how weak you were."

"That's over now," I said.

"I sensed someone watching me, in Cape Misfortune, before I was kidnapped. A seer from the Imperia. Wessendorf has a group of psychic dead people on the payroll. A manna tunnel opened in my bedroom."

"Aggie, we all missed you."

"How are Mom and Dad?"

"Mom is good. Dad went missing," I said.

Aggie looked down at the sand.

"I dreamt he was in the Stitching Factory."

She picked up a handful of sand and let it trickle out through her fingers.

"I'm going to destroy the Imperia."

"How are you going to do that?" Elliott asked.

"Use their own weapons against them. Destroy the burn supply."

"How?" I said.

"The Imperia refine manna all over this world and pipe all of it to the Winter Garden, their capital, out at sea. They have a reservoir there. That's where we'll hit them."

We were quiet for a minute.

"I'm not going home until I've blown the Imperia up," Aggie said.

Elliott smiled.

"The Dollar sisters."

Later, we walked towards the coast in the cool of a desert evening, under a star-freckled sky. There was a buzzing noise. Something dark in the air, flying low.

"Diesel and burn engine. A slave-catcher," Aggie said.

A searchlight snapped on. A circle of bright light played over the sand.

We ran, but there was no cover. Ropes fell out of a metal gondola and trailed on the sand. Four shadowy figures climbed down.

Three wore ragged clothes and carried rifles with bayonets fixed on the end. One held a pistol and wore a three-piece suit.

"Good evening," he said. "I am Lieutenant Jäger of the Imperia Marine Company. I am a licensed slave taker."

He had a drooping mustache and wore a western-style gun belt on his hip. The ragged men grabbed Elliott and took his rifle.

"Hold the females," Jäger said.

One of them held me. His grip was superhuman.

He unfurled a leather roll filled with steel instruments.

"Leave them alone," Elliott said.

Jäger took out a syringe.

"You're going to be cut into pieces to work for the Imperia, my fine strong lad."

"Is that right?" Elliott said.

Jäger stuck the syringe in Aggie's arm and drew blood. He squirted the red liquid into a metal instrument that looked like an oversized pocket watch. He repeated the procedure on me.

"Saturated with juice."

The ragged crew grinned and clapped each other on the back. Jäger looked at us.

"We're going to climb up into the big bird. Halfway up, you may feel a desire to jump off and make a run for it. Believe me, you wouldn't be the first. But we are all hand-picked men. We'll catch you again and kill you, even if it means missing out on a few pennies."

"How long have you been dead, Lieutenant?" Aggie asked.

He thought for a moment.

"It's more than a hundred years since I took the new life, if that's what you mean."

"In that long time, did it never bother you how many people were pressed to death, so you could live your stupid zombie life?"

He shook his head.

"Honestly? No. It's just the way the dice falls. Soon, manna cows like you will be redundant. There are big, widow-maker drills on the sea floor sucking manna up from the earth now."

I looked up at the dark airship silhouetted against the stars.

"Up we go - one, two, three like happy monkeys up a tree," one of the crew said.

The ropes were knotted to make climbing easier. It was slow going. I felt waves of despair the higher we got.

Then something came out of the night. It scrambled up my rope with swift, supernatural strength. Lieutenant Jäger, a few feet below me, shot his pistol. It didn't stop the shadow, who climbed up and bit out the man's jugular, spraying the night air with luminous blood. Jäger fell noiselessly to the ground.

The wolf leaped onto Elliott's rope and bit out the crewman's neck. I saw Elliott wrestle his rifle from the sailor, before he kicked him into the darkness.

The man below Aggie had his rifle and bayonet ready, trying to stab the wolf as it bit him. The weapon fell into the night, followed by its owner. The last sailor jumped off without a fight.

The creature, in the shadows, jumped onto my rope and the silhouette changed into the shape of a man. Mr. Winterbeard climbed up, pulling on his hospital uniform over a chest covered in glowing blood.

"If I had really died, you would have forgotten me completely. It would be as if I never existed. That is the nature of sacrifice here. We call it a disappearance. But your sister wasn't dead - neither am I."

"How did you find us?"

"I'm a wolf. I followed your scent."

"Of course."

"Let's take this slave boat," Elliott said.

The airship's steel gondola had a wheelhouse cabin at the bow. A brass plaque on the door said, 'The Little Warlord.'

Inside it, a tall, unshaven man wearing a grubby, white suit and red bowtie sat behind the wheel. He had a half-empty bottle of burn in his hand.

A small, blue-skinned man sat on the floor. He wore glasses, and had an iron collar around his neck. His wings had been cut off, leaving bony stubs protruding from his shoulders. A square hole in the steel wall allowed him to touch the wooden hull. He looked up in alarm. Then he smiled.

"Was your mission a success, Mr. Jäger?" the tall man asked.

"Mr. Jäger won't be joining us," I said.

The man turned. He looked astonished. Then he recovered himself.

"Rascals like you are always brought to justice. There is no escape from the College of Seers. The Imperia will hunt you down."

Mr. Winterbeard opened the wheelhouse window, grabbed the man's belt and shirt collar and threw him into the night.

The bullet and stab wounds in the old wolf man's chest leaked glowing liquid.

"How long have you been dead, Mr. Winterbeard?" I asked.

"A long while. Some of us were greedy for the immortality Wessendorf promised. You soon learned it took a quarter pint of burn a day to stay alive. So, we were slaves."

Mr. Winterbeard held up a ring of keys and opened a cabinet on the wall, revealing two racks of bright orange bottles. He pulled the cork out of one and drank greedily. The wounds showing through his torn tunic scabbed over and disappeared.

"Are there many like you? Undead wolves?"

"Not from my tribe, most refused and were killed. I was the chief."

Elliott patted Mr. Winterbeard on the back.

"We couldn't have got this far without you. I hope you carry on redeeming yourself."

The Little Warlord sailed across the dark desert. Aggie, Elliott and I stood on the deck watching the sand dunes go past. The little, blue man walked out polishing his glasses, and breathing in the night air.

"My name is Mr. Augustus Pemm. I have been a prisoner aboard this ship for thirty-six years."

He saw me looking at the stubs on his shoulders.

"They will grow back, given time, as everything did here when the manna flowed. Who knows, with enough burn, I may fly again, over the forest, as I have done so often in my dreams."

He sat on a slave bench, pushing the manacles onto the floor. Then he drank from a glowing bottle.

"Do you know how to get to the Winter Garden?" Aggie asked.

"Not a place any sane person would want to go to, if you don't mind my observing. What do you want to do there?"

"Have a reckoning," my sister said.

"Ah. Something every slave dreams of."

"And every vengeful ghost," a voice said, barely louder than the wind whistling in the ship's balloon rigging.

Charlie stood amongst the shadows in the ship's stern, his bike beside him. His flickering, spectral body cast a faint, baleful light over the deck.

I walked over. He touched my arm. His ghostly fingers were cold.

"I came here to tell you something, Cassie. There are infinite worlds, but only one afterlife. Hang on to that."

"I don't understand."

"You will."

His body faded, then flickered back into definition.

"You may need to enlist the help of an old friend. Oh, and I spoke to the storm maidens for you - I'm dead, but they can still hear my song. I've used all my energy. I can't help anyone anymore."

"You've done more than enough, Charlie," Aggie said.

Charlie nodded. Then he was blown away by the wind.

"We've got company. Ship on the horizon!" Elliott shouted.

A long, steel tube, with stabilizing fins at one end, whistled out of the darkness and drew level with us.

Elliott shot at it. The explosion knocked us onto the deck.

"Nice shooting," I said.

"That was a rocket. They're firing ranging shots," he said.

I ran into the wheelhouse. Mr. Winterbeard was studying a chart. Mr. Pemm sat with his hand on the boat.

"The Warlord doesn't like this at all," he said.

"We need to go," I said.

"Where?" Mr. Pemm said.

"Into the drink."

There was an explosion on the deck. Black smoke blew in through the wheelhouse door. A rocket hit the steel cabin. Glass and orange flames exploded around us.

"Take us down, Mr. Pemm," Mr. Winterbeard ordered.

"She's going down anyway."

On the deck, Mr. Winterbeard handed out gillyflower leaves. Smoke billowed from the stern.

Our pursuers were so close, I saw a man in a peaked cap giving orders on the warship's deck. Half a dozen rockets flew towards us.

I pulled a splinter of wood from Elliott's cheek and stuck a red leaf in his mouth. There were three explosions at the stern, one after another. The boat turned on its side. We rolled down the deck, hit the ship's rail and bounced into the air. I saw Aggie put a gillyleaf between her teeth and give the thumbs up. Then she was gone.

Elliott grabbed my hand. Below us, I saw the foaming crests of high waves. We splashed into bubbling water. The Little Warlord, now a ball of flame, plunged into the sea behind us.

Three black forms moved swiftly towards us.

"Thank you for rescuing us, Light in Water," I said, climbing onto the storm maiden's neck.

"When the manna was plentiful, we flew in the air," a voice in my head said. "We changed shape into many different forms – birds, bears, horses, even fae. Now, we can only fly beneath the water."

"The Dollar sisters are changers. Bathed in the manna fog," Mr. Winterbeard said, from behind us.

"Everyone is a changer. Even you, young man," the storm maiden said to Elliott. "The coast guard who dared to swim between worlds."

The shadow of our pursuers broke up the moonlight reflected on the water's surface. They didn't find us.

Chapter Nine
An Old Friend

The Storm Maiden's long horns cut holes in the ice fringing the southern shores of Winterland.

We traveled through a pine forest to a rocky waterfall deep in enemy territory. Then we walked through a watery curtain to one of the ancient tunnels that honeycombed the mountain. We came to a dark space. These caves were sacred places, even now damp with manna, where wolves had learned to change their form into that of their enemy, man.

"Summoning the dead was quite matter-of-fact in our pack," Mr. Winterbeard said. "Although always something to be undertaken cautiously."

Five of us stood around a deep, circular bowl. A drop of manna fell from the ragged roof and trickled down the side of the cavity. The pit below us was filled with glowing liquid. Mr. Winterbeard held out his hand. I gave him Ed's bullet necklace, which had snapped off in my hand on the Andiamo.

Mr. Winterbeard dropped it into the basin, which flared with green flames so bright they were hard to look at. When they died down, a grisly figure stood in the bowl. Glowing tattoos flickered above a tortured mass of sinew and muscle.

"Hey, Ed," I said. "How's the afterlife working out for you?"

A gob of dark spit dribbled over the surviving left half of his jawbone, splattering onto the basin.

"Cassie. And your boyfriend. How I dearly wish I'd killed you both."

"You tried," Elliott said.

"You cheated."

The skull turned to Aggie.

"You must be the missing twin – no doubt the second most annoying bitch in the universe."

That made Aggie smile.

"We need information, Ed," I said.

"So, the guts of a crocosaurus. After a while the stomach juices burn your skin off, followed by the soft tissue and muscle. Later it burns your eyes out. And you realize, this is it. No one's coming for you. This is how you disappear forever. All because of Deputy Cassie Dollar!"

His entire jaw bone fell off. He caught it and stuck it back in.

"I need your help," I said.

He held up a bony finger.

"I want my body back. Nothing less. With a hundred gallons of burn. And the *Andiamo.*"

"The *Andiamo* sank," I said.

"If the Imperia seers find out you have been in contact with us, they will end you. Help us, and we won't tell them," Aggie said.

"Blackmail," Ed said. "A language I understand. You can tell you're Cassandra's twin. Like her, you're incredibly annoying."

I looked at Mr. Winterbeard across manna-laced flames. He shrugged.

"It's possible. My tribe performed the restoration ceremony on corpses brought back to face punishment."

"Cash on delivery, Edwyn," I said. "We succeed - you get your body back."

"Who's the old guy?"

"My name is Mr. Cecil Winterbeard."

"A mangy, old wolf. You're the guy who is getting my body back?"

Ed spat another defiant gob which puffed on the basin edge.

"Okay, what do you want to know?" he said.

"The explosives you used on the roof," I said. "Forensics thought you had a bomb factory somewhere."

"You thinking of blowing something up, darling?"

"Oh yeah."

"You've come to the right guy."

Chapter Ten
Narwak

We dived into warm, treacly currents. A strong tide dragged us into a colder ocean. A shadow passed over the water, like a bird of prey landing. Then the gillyleaves between our teeth shriveled.

We surfaced in a different world. The dark cliffs around Wish Bay were a line on the horizon. We wouldn't last long in these waters, we both knew, so we didn't hang around.

We came out of the surf and climbed the steps to the cliff top.

I had worked out it was probably a week day evening, maybe Tuesday or Wednesday, so the little Needlepoint station would be uncrewed.

We arrived a few minutes before the end of shift and watched Ann drive off in her car.

I punched in the entry code. Inside, we took off our sodden clothes and took a hot shower.

I changed into my spare uniform. Elliott donned some military-style, black clothes from the riot gear locker.

The keys to the patrol car were still in my gear belt – a survivor of my trip to another world. I checked the weather on the car's computer. The weasel fog would last until round about midnight. That didn't leave us much time.

We sped across the salt marshes towards Slaughter Lake.

The newly-opened Coffi Spa was a sleek square of dark glass and polished sandstone that sat smugly on the waterfront. There was another Sheriff's Office SUV in the parking lot.

A young woman, who from her small stature might have been fae, sat behind a white reception desk.

"Sorry, the spa is closed," she said.

I showed her my ID.

"I need to see the Sheriff."

"He's finishing up in one of the executive treatment rooms."

"Where are they?"

She hesitated.

"It's an emergency."

"Downstairs."

Sheriff Frederson lay on a padded massage table with a cigarette in one hand and an empty champagne glass he was using as an ashtray in the other.

He didn't look pleased to see us.

"You've got a hell of a nerve barging in here," he said, grabbing a towel. "I'm going to make sure you spend the rest of your life in jail for murder."

"Ed Henderson said you would be here. He sends his regards, by the way," I said.

"Henderson is dead, although you may have missed that when you were fleeing the crime scene."

"We need some info, Hank, then we'll be on our way," I said.

"Where's the bomb factory?" Elliott said.

"I have no idea what you are talking about. Why ask me?"

"Edwyn says you're in charge of things on the Cape."

Hank sat up on his bed and pointed at me.

"We have evidence linking you with the murder of Boone Washienko, Dame Teddy Champion, Bliss Schneider and volunteer deputy, Karl Rieper."

"Make a phone call to Ed's brother, Glad," Elliott said.

Hank crossed his arms.

"Never heard of him."

I walked over, stuck a Glock under Hank's chin and pulled the trigger.

Glowing brains hit the ceiling and dripped down onto the massage bed. Hank's eyes rolled back. He slid off the table.

A few seconds later his eyes rolled forward.

"Where is Glad Henderson, Sheriff?" I said.

He focused on my face.

"You are so far out of your depth, honey. There's nothing you can do to me. As you've seen, I'm already dead."

"I'll cut your head off and throw it in the lake," Elliott said.

Hank held up a hand.

"Narwak rock. In the lighthouse keeper's lodge."

"Thank you. You're a disgrace to your uniform, Hank," I said.

"I was sick. They offered me a new life."

"Tell Glad we want everything he's got. Tell him to get it ready."

We trussed Sheriff Frederson up and put him in the trunk, later transferring him to the kayak onboard the Mud Hen. Elliott piloted us through thick fog to a dark and silent Narwak rock.

"We have ten minutes here, tops," he said.

The door to the keeper's lodge was open. A hunched figure sat at a small table, reading a magazine in the light of a candle.

I held up a shotgun I had taken from the Needlepoint safe.

"You Glad Henderson?"

The man looked up. For a second, I thought it was Ed, but this man was older and looked outwardly respectable.

"Where's Hank?" he asked.

"Tied up."

"In answer to your question, I am Glad. But not glad to meet you. Could you stop pointing that thing at me, Officer? I'm unarmed."

He held up his hands. Elliott walked behind him and took a pearl-handled automatic from the man's jeans waistband.

"Hank gave you up. We're here for the explosives," I said. "And, we're in a hurry."

"The TV news did a piece on your commemoration service a couple of days ago. Not a great turnout from your fellow officers."

"We're in a hurry," Elliott said.

Glad turned to him.

"And who might you be, friend?"

"Coast Guard."

"We need everything you've got," I said.

"Flattered I still have anything a young woman would be interested in," he said, with a chuckle.

"I want what's hidden in the wall of your cellar. A little birdie told us you had plastique, anti-personnel mines, firing systems, detonators," I said.

He stopped smiling.

"They were mistaken. Are you two part of that Satanism thing Ed got into?"

"Stop wasting time," I said.

"They'll kill me."

"We'll kill you," I said.

I saw Hank's face in one of the room's broken windows. A handgun fired twice.

Elliott and I flattened ourselves.

Glad held his shin.

"You shot me, Hank, you idiot. That's just perfect," he said.

"I've called for help," Hank shouted. "Valkyrie Marine Service and a chopper are on their way."

"Get the explosives," Elliott said, taking the shotgun. "I'll hold the fort."

I took out a knife and put it against Glad's back. He opened the padlock on an old, wooden door and hopped down some stairs.

It was a square, brick room that felt damp and looked completely empty. Glad took a wrecking bar off a nail banged into a ceiling joist, stuck one end into the wall and grunted. A square section fell off, revealing two oversized backpacks.

"Great working with you, Glad," I said.

"A real pleasure, Deputy."

I padlocked the door.

Elliott lay on the kitchen floor in a pool of blood. There was a bullet in his thigh.

Hank's headless body lay on the floor.

"We had an altercation," Elliott said.

I dragged Hank's body over the cliff and pulled Elliott to his feet. He cried out, and I put him back down.

"I need a hospital. You'll have to leave me," he said.

"What? No."

He pushed me away.

"I love you," I said.

But he didn't answer. His eyes closed and his head slumped.

I hauled the two backpacks onto the Mud Hen and started the engine.

I saw the lights of a chopper over the headland.

The fog looked far out at sea now.

I pushed the throttle up to full and turned the boat North-Northwest and sped out towards the thickening fog.

Part III: The City of the Dead

Chapter One
The Lake

I thought of the tall tales Grandma told us. She claimed they were hogwash. Maybe they were preparation.

I felt dizzy and wondered if I was just some crazy murder suspect driving a boat in the fog.

Salt spray *tap-tapped* on the cracked cabin window. The wind outside moaned. Together, they were a harmony. A shadow passed over the boat. There was a creaking sound - like a rope stretching tight.

The gillyleaf I had placed beside the ship's wheel un-withered into waxy health.

I turned the engine off.

Aggie pulled herself over the side.

"How did it go?"

"I got the equipment."

"Where's Elliott?"

"Hurt."

"Badly?"

"He got shot. I love him, Aggie."

She patted me on the shoulder.

"He's a determined guy. He came all the way over here to get you. I'm sure he'll try his hardest to be okay."

"I hope so."

"Let's save the world so that I can be maid of honor at your wedding."

She held up an imaginary champagne glass.

"I already have one failed marriage," I said.

She pretended to down the drink and threw the glass overboard.

"Well, here's to second chances."

Mr. Pemm climbed in, followed a second later by a sodden Mr. Winterbeard, water streaming from his long beard.

"Light in the water sends her good wishes," he said.

"You're going to need them where we're going," Aggie said.

Mr. Pemm navigated. We sailed around the Winterland pack ice for the best part of a week.

We beached the Mud Hen in an icy cove on the outskirts of an industrial port. Steam-driven distilleries dominated the town's skyline.

Our party trudged across soot-grimed snow.

We came to a twenty foot high, metal pipe that came out of the distilleries and disappeared into the ice. A winged man with a Kalashnikov rifle slung over his shoulder patrolled on the beach.

A wolf jumped up behind him. Luminous blood sprayed across the snow.

Aggie set a digital timer on a brick of plastic explosive using a laminated, instruction booklet.

Mr. Winterbeard climbed a ladder and opened an access hatch. He and Mr. Pemm dropped into flowing luminous liquid.

Aggie clung to an oversized backpack.

"Here goes nothing," she said, putting a gillyleaf in her mouth and splashing into the burn.

I hugged my bag and jumped after her. Burn closed over my head.

The air coming through the gillyleaf tasted like a cough candy and diesel.

The pipe inclined downwards for a few hundred feet before leveling out on the seabed. Soon, we were traveling fast. The Winter Garden was eighteen miles out. It wouldn't take long at this rate.

The liquid around me seeped into my skin. I saw vivid images of other places. I saw Grandma, still alive in a different time, drinking cranberry wine. I saw wolf cubs playing in the snow. They were the memories of Mr. Winterbeard. I had a vision of Aggie in her bedroom fighting with Eugene Kard. I saw a surgeon clamping folds of flesh around the wound in Elliott's thigh. I saw Mr. Winterbeard on his knees pleading with grinning, Imperia goons as they set fire to the houses in his village. I saw Mr. Pemm and a line of fae having their wings sawn off. I saw Boone, with no shoes and a collar around his neck, serving drinks to a man and a woman in a marble tub. His eyes were lifeless.

The pipe went upwards. I saw a memory; I couldn't tell if it was mine or Aggie's, of Grandma saying, "I'll always be in your corner, girls."

"Burn the burn," my father's voice said.

The pressure slackened. The liquid lowered until we were kneeling in an empty pipe.

Aggie stood up.

"Looks like the plastique worked."

Our dip in the glowing liquid had agreed with Mr. Winterbeard. His long beard had turned copper-colored.

"I've drunk more burn today than in a century," he said.

He punched the side of the pipe. It left a fist-shaped indentation. Ahead of us, Mr. Pemm was examining a new pair of wings.

Only a single rivulet of glowing liquid lay at the bottom of the pipe now.

We walked until a white pinprick of light grew into a circle of daylight. Then we were at the end of the pipe, looking out.

A vast reservoir of shimmering burn lay ahead of us, a lake of swirling incandescent light that stretched into infinity.

Mr. Pemm stared out in wonder.

"I thought this place was a myth. The newsreels always said burn is in short supply."

"This will feed a lot of dead people," I said.

"An army," Mr. Pemm said, jumping in.

"Well, tally ho, chaps," Aggie said, biting on her gillyleaf and dropping into the glowing sea beneath.

I plunged down to where my twin sister hung suspended in the light. Mr. Winterbeard dropped down beside us.

It was almost too bright to see anything.

I saw the image of a tree whose branches connected other worlds and times. The leaves fed it light and nourishment. Manna was the sap. Then I saw a dead army climbing down the branches.

"Not going to happen," a faint voice said. "Not with the Dollar sisters on the case."

Aggie gave me a thumbs-up.

"Can you hear what I'm thinking?" I thought, to myself.

She nodded.

"I can. Evidently, burn doesn't just affect dead people."

The exposure was still changing Mr. Winterbeard. He looked like a young man now. Mr. Pemm was using his wings to swoop around under the water.

We swam most of the morning, stopping when we saw the side of the reservoir.

Then we were suspended for hours, washed in a strange light, having little visions, until a shadow moved above us.

Julius Wessendorf's private train pulled up.

"Charlie said it picks up a private supply of burn for Wessendorf and his cronies and takes it inside the palace walls," Aggie thought.

We floated upwards to a few feet below the reservoir's surface.

A hoist lifted a long, steel, freight car over the bright lake and dropped it in.

When it sank below the surface, we swam in through the open top and twirled amongst eddying liquid. Then two roof flaps shut over us with a bang.

The hoist swung the receptacle onto the train. The clickety-clack of wheels on rails echoed through the bright, viscous liquid.

Mr. Winterbeard pointed to a hatch in the car roof.

We lay down on top of the freight car while a warm wind dried off our bodies.

"So, this is the Wintergarden," I said.

"It's a greenhouse," Aggie said.

A curved ceiling of glass extended half a mile up. Birds flew under it.

"I feel so alive," Mr. Winterbeard said. "No wonder the powers that be keep everyone on strict rations."

"While drinking buckets themselves no doubt," Mr. Pemm said, licking some last burn from the back of his hand.

The foliage on either side of the train was lush and tropical. We passed fields of pineapple, mango, maize, and cowpeas. There were cattle, too. I saw a bunch of cows munching on hay bales.

With a glass roof, there would be no rain. All irrigation, courtesy of Wessendorf, I thought.

There were icebergs visible beyond the glass. But here the air was warm and humid.

A line of dirty wooden shacks went by.

"Thanks for coming to get me, Cassie," Aggie said.

"Sorry it took so long. Wish I could have saved Dad."

"You can still go back to Cape Misfortune, you know."

"I think this job will require both Dollar sisters," I said.

Ahead of us, a high, stone wall snaked around a mountain.

"It's claimed the mortar in the city wall is made from the ground up bones of vanquished enemies," Mr. Pemm said.

Six tall towers, beyond the wall, loomed above ancient, Rome-style temples and palaces. The marble that covered them was blood red.

Men in black uniforms marched along tree-lined streets.

"This was an island before the Imperia came," Mr. Pemm said. "A holy place of fire and mystery that rose from the sea. The home of our old gods. Now it is a glass coffin."

Mr. Pemm pointed to a square in the center of the city.

"I was traded there twice. I labored in the silver mines, beneath the mountain here, for a spoonful of burn a day. One day, a supervisor noticed my navigation skills in the tunnels, so I was sold to a slave ship."

"The seers are near," Mr. Winterbeard said. "Close your minds if you suspect an unwanted visitor."

On the journey around the coast, Aggie had taught me to imagine a brick wall around my thoughts.

As we drew closer, I could see the black, uniformed soldiers perpetually march through the city, carrying silver Kalashnikov rifles and long sabers. Something sparkled on belts they wore across their chests.

"The silver beaker," Mr. Winterbeard said. "The half-pint, double ration for the brave men and women who fight for the Imperia."

The blue man flapped his wings.

"Shall we go?" He said.

"Where?" Aggie asked.

"Somewhere only birds or the fae can go, Miss Agata."

Chapter Two
Imperia

"Can we ever escape where we come from?" Grandma once asked Aggie and me.

I don't think she meant geography. But, maybe, I should have left the Cape far behind. Something kept me. I worked hard. I didn't cause a fuss about Aggie or Dad. I was a good wife. I allowed myself to hope for the future. But I couldn't ignore myself.

Now I clung to the back of a winged fae above a cruel, terrifying city. It felt like I had been headed here since the day Aggie went missing.

Mr. Pemm ferried us to a flat, circular floor carved in the rock, high up in the mountain above Imperia.

"How long can a dead person last without burn?" Aggie asked, as we sat on the floor and prepared explosives.

"A day and a night before they...we...stop moving," Mr. Winterbeard said. "And another few before our bodies become husks."

"But we still think, our souls live in dreams," Mr. Pemm said. "An absence – perpetually waiting. That is the fate of the gods who once lived in these mountains."

"I've heard the cries of those old ones," Aggie said.

"They were betrayed by one of their own, Krampus. Wessendorf is his Lieutenant," Mr. Winterbeard said.

"The one who betrayed the others?" I said. "Is he here in Imperia?"

"No one has ever seen him."

"So, what will happen to you two after this?" Aggie said.

Mr. Pemm and Mr. Winterbeard looked at each other.

"If your plan succeeds the storm maidens have offered us some manna. It will keep us alive, or dead, for a while," the old wolfman said.

Mr. Pemm then told us of the early days of the city below us. Many of the Imperia aristocrats, in his tales, had the same surnames as the Cape's founding fathers - the impoverished immigrants, if you believed the legend, who transformed a Pacific wilderness into a thriving center of lumber and coal.

"Now they spend their time hunting people in the reforested woods or gambling their immense wealth at cards."

Later that afternoon, Aggie and I sat on the grassy shores of the burn reservoir, laying out explosives in the dying sunlight.

Aggie held up an oversized, black brick with six bug-like arms.

"Italian limpet mine. Complete with suction cups and nail shooters. We have six," she said, holding up a laminated instruction book. "The instructions are in Italian, but the diagrams are pretty good – easier than IKEA."

I taped blocks of plastic explosive together.

"Your basic underwater high-end, plastic-bonded explosive," I said.

"The reservoir of burn is ultimately held up by leg struts," Mr. Pemm said.

"So, if we hit the right place, it will open up like a tin can?" Aggie asked.

"The Lake of the Dead will empty into the sea, where it will quickly be rendered unusable."

Aggie whistled.

"What would we do without Mr. Pemm?" she said.

The little man smiled uncertainly.

"Good luck."

We dived into the shining honey.

The burn seeped into my skin. I saw Eugene Kard's wife lying on the floor of his apartment in Portland. I saw the souls of Uncle Buzz and Charlie rise from their bodies in the attic room of the old Wessendorf house.

We arranged the explosives along the seam between two steel plates. I set the limpet mine fire-delay to an hour.

"We're ready," I thought.

I climbed out of the reservoir and swung my near-empty bag onto the bank.

"Now for the diversion," I said, giving Aggie and Mr. Winterbeard a small hug. "Mr. Pemm and I will be back in a few minutes if all goes well. Otherwise, get to the Mud Hen and meet with the storm maidens."

The blue-skinned man put his arm around my waist.

"How long before your bombs go off, my dear?" he asked, as we rose up beside the city wall.

Maybe it was the way he asked. For some reason, I don't know why, I lied.

"Three-quarters of an hour."

I heard Boone's wedding ring rattle in my gear belt.

We flew over the red city towards the tallest of the six towers, which had a decorative iron skull at the top.

Mr. Pemm landed in the left eye cavity, which overlooked a lush roof garden.

Boone stood quietly, looking out over the city. He wore a tuxedo. His right hand held a silver tray. It had a bottle of champagne with two glasses on it.

I stuck a detonator in a brick of plastique and dropped it on the floor. We flew down to Boone. I took his ring out. It jumped out of my hand and rolled to his feet.

"Time we got you home," I said.

He turned towards me. His eyes were glassy.

"Run," he said.

Then I heard a polite cough behind me.

I turned and saw a man I had only seen in old, Victorian photographs –heavily built, dark hair, a glossy beard. He wore his trademark stovepipe hat.

"Hello, Cassandra Dollar," Julius Wessendorf said. "And, thank you to Mr. Pemm. You will be free to go once you bring me the sister."

"I didn't want to die," the blue-skinned man said to me with an apologetic shrug.

"Mr. Pemm has informed us about the explosives." Julius's voice had a slight European accent.

Mr. Pemm flew up to the eye cavity and took the explosives, before flying into the gathering night.

"Well, this has all been very successful. You caused me a few problems, but thankfully Cape Misfortune is full of weak people. Two glasses of French champagne, Boone," Wessendorf said. "All the way from across the worlds."

He sipped.

"You intrigue me. Would you like to live forever?"

"If it means associating with people like you, no thanks."

I looked at the red sun setting through the city's far-off, glass roof.

"You know how I got started on all this? At sunset," Wessendorf said. "I heard the fae store the light of the dying sun in their eyes. That's how to tell they're not human. I caught one in Cape Misfortune."

"Now you have a zombie empire."

He took another sip.

"I have my own private, manna extractor here. And a mini-distillery. I like to drink burn fresh. It tastes better. I'm going to press your twin sister until she dies. And then I'm going to press you."

Mr. Pemm dropped down with Agata struggling in his arms.

"Please, leave my sister alone," I said.

Wessendorf raised an eyebrow and sang a little snatch of a song – "Into each life some rain must fall."

I looked at Boone. There were beads of sweat on his forehead.

Two soldiers appeared and dragged Aggie to a metal room without a roof where they strapped her into a high-backed chair.

"Please," I said. "Do what you want to me, but let her go."

"What sort of a name is Dollar, anyway?" Wessendorf asked. "It's not Cape."

"It's Italian. My grandfather. Please don't do this."

"I went on a grand tour of Italy as a young man. I do so adore the Roman Empire. I see my work as a continuation of the Imperial ideal. I'll make myself Emperor. My mentor, Krampus, can be pope – he loves all the religious bunkum."

This can't be happening, I thought. We were so close. Make this a dream. A bad dream.

"Please, Julius, Mr. Wessendorf."

"I never really liked America, or the pioneer experience. We were too much like barbarians."

My sister's body arched in the air. She let out a prolonged scream. Then she was still.

"No coming back from that," Wessendorf said. "The truth is your sister disappeared a long time ago."

Boone was staring at Wessendorf now. He picked up the gold ring at his feet and put it on.

Julius filled a silver beaker from a tap beside Aggie's chair. He raised it to me.

"Here's to infinite worlds and never-ending conquest."

"Goodbye, Cass," Boone said.

He charged the soldiers. All three went over the side of the roof.

Wessendorf laughed.

I hoped we had timed things right. I ran towards him. A distant explosion shook the building, knocking us both over.

Mr. Pemm swooped out of the sky with a saber in his hand.

"Mr. Pemm," Julius said.

The sword separated Wessendorf's head from his body. It rolled over the terrace into the city of the dead.

I unstrapped Aggie from the chair.

"He's killed her. She's really dead," I said.

I sank to my knees.

"It was all for nothing."

"Not necessarily," Mr. Winterbeard said, from the eye socket. "You have defeated the Imperia."

"Aggie could be saved," Mr. Pemm said, "with burn."

"I don't want her to be a zombie, Augustus. She wouldn't want that either."

"Then there must be a sacrifice," Mr. Winterbeard said.

Chapter Three
The Price

M r. Pemm flew us to the city in the desert.

"There is a price to pay for all change," the Queen of Stars said, once the hidden temple had risen from the sand. "Take a life to save a life. That's the rule."

We laid Aggie's body on the stone altar.

"I can't stand sacrifice twice. The rule is one for one," Mr. Winterbeard said.

"I will," I said.

"So be it. One sister for another. Someone loses. Someone wins. It will be as if you never existed. No-one will know of your life or disappearance. Will you still stand sacrifice, Cassandra Dollar?"

"Yes," I said.

Epilogue

My name is Agata Dollar. I am a Sheriff's deputy on the southern coast of Oregon. I grew up on a cranberry farm owned by my Mom and Dad. I suppose I'm as lucky as anyone can be in this world. I finished high school and married a good man named Boone. I count my blessings every day.

Most evenings, when I finish my shift, I like to take a walk over the rocks of Wish Bay. I love this stretch of shore. The ocean is beautiful - although up close, cold and pitiless.

Sometimes the surf breaks on the rocks and I hear, faintly, the whisper of someone close to me, whose words I can't quite catch. I look around the beach and think to myself - I am alone here.

Then, for some reason, I think of my twin sister who was born dead after I was delivered safely. Cassandra, my mother wanted to call her.

I sometimes dream that Cassandra also grew up in this place and loved it as much as I did.

Most nights, on my walk, I hear her voice in the surf, calling to me.

The police psychiatrist, Teddy Champion, thinks it's the stress of the job. She advises me to take my evening walks somewhere else.

But I think all is not well in Cape Misfortune.

Why do I hear Cassandra's voice when she never had one?

The ghost of a tired man, called the Levitator, visited my dreams and said there are many worlds where events happened differently, but only one afterlife. So, my twin Cassandra may still exist, somewhere.

Once I heard the surf say, "No one really disappears if they know where they are."

Postscript

My father found a manuscript on the farm's back porch, left during the fog. The paper is bleached, the handwriting so faint you can hardly read it. It is a strange story called "Cape Misfortune, or the Disappearance of Cassandra Dollar." The author claims to be my long dead twin.

If what she says is true Cape Misfortune is in peril. It will need two Dollar sisters. I will find her.

END

About Henry Anderson

Henry Anderson is a former news reporter who has written for national UK newspapers. He studied English at Oxford. He spent time as a farmhand in Australia before working in publishing and journalism. His first novel "The Mouth" is published by Solstice.

Social Media

Website and blog https://henryandersonbooks.com

Twitter https://twitter.com/macandersauthor

Facebook https://www.facebook.com/henryandersonauthor

Instagram: https://www.instagram.com/macanderz

Amazon Author Page: http://author.to/henryanderson

Acknowledgements

Thanks to Justin for sharing his law enforcement knowledge.

If you enjoyed this story, check out these other Solstice Publishing books by Henry Anderson:

The Mouth

When Jack's home town is burned down his mortally-wounded grandfather tells him of a device called "The Mouth" that opens doors into other worlds.

He must do the impossible - find the world that gave his enemies their extraordinary power and travel to an England known simply as "The Maximum."

The Mouth is a science-fantasy adventure story about hope, resolve and finding the courage to carry on fighting even when all seems lost.

46821246R00146

Made in the USA
Middletown, DE
01 June 2019